I0650314

Bartholomew S. De Forest

Random Sketches and Wandering Thoughts

What I saw in camp, on the march, the bivouac, the battle field and hospital, while

with the Army in Virginia, North and South Carolina, during the late rebellion

Bartholomew S. De Forest

Random Sketches and Wandering Thoughts
What I saw in camp, on the march, the bivouac, the battle field and hospital, while with the
Army in Virginia, North and South Carolina, during the late rebellion

ISBN/EAN: 9783337194970

Printed in Europe, USA, Canada, Australia, Japan

Cover: Foto ©Andreas Hilbeck / pixelio.de

More available books at **www.hansebooks.com**

RANDOM SKETCHES

AND

WANDERING THOUGHTS;

OR,

WHAT I SAW IN CAMP, ON THE MARCH, THE BIVOUAC, THE
BATTLE FIELD AND HOSPITAL, WHILE WITH THE
ARMY IN VIRGINIA, NORTH AND SOUTH
CAROLINA, DURING THE LATE
REBELLION.

WITH A HISTORICAL-SKETCH OF

THE SECOND OSWEGO REGIMENT,

EIGHTY-FIRST NEW YORK STATE V. I.;

A RECORD OF ALL ITS OFFICERS, AND ROSTER OF ITS
ENLISTED MEN; ALSO, AN APPENDIX.

BY B. S. DE FOREST,

LATE FIRST LIEUTENANT AND R. Q. M.

Brevet-Major.

ALBANY, N. Y.:

AVERY HERRICK, PUBLISHER.

1866.

Entered according to Act of Congress, in the year 1866, by

B. S. De Forest,

In the Clerk's Office of the District Court of the United States, for the
Northern District of New York.

AVERY HERRICK,
PRINTER AND STEREOTYPER,
NO. 496 BROADWAY,
ALBANY N. Y.

TO THE VOLUNTEER SOLDIERS

OF THE

LATE UNION ARMY,

FOR THEIR PATRIOTISM, COURAGE AND FORTITUDE,

IN THE HOUR OF OUR COUNTRY'S TRIAL,

WHO STOOD AS A LIVING WALL

BETWEEN FREEDOM AND DESPOTISM,

THIS VOLUME IS

RESPECTFULLY DEDICATED.

PREFACE.

When these RANDOM SKETCHES AND WANDERING THOUGHTS were written, the Author had no idea of having them published. They were first a memoranda of events which transpired from day to day, in camp and on the march, which was kept in a small field book, in which was also noted such reflections as suggested themselves at the time. The manuscript was looked upon as a sort of reserve fund upon which to draw for light reading, when it could not be obtained from any other source, with which to amuse himself and relieve the tedium of camp life; also as a record for refreshing his memory in after years, in regard to the leading incidents of the great struggle we were then passing through. On reading some of the manuscript to friends in whose judgment he had confidence, he has been induced to have it published in book form.

People who are loyal, and appreciate sentiments flowing from a patriotic heart, and those who think well of the soldier, who left the comforts of home to share in the dangers and privations of the battle field and camp, may read and be entertained by it. They will doubtless find that it contains faults, if they choose

*1

to look for them. It does not challenge criticism, it makes no special pretension to literary merit, but simply gives an unvarnished description of soldier life in the field, and what the writer saw in the South, as it presented itself to his mind at the time.

The history of the Second Oswego Regiment, (81st New York State Veteran Volunteer Infantry,) other than of his own knowledge, was obtained from various reliable sources, and it is thought would be interesting to many, in connection with the Sketch Book, especially to those who belonged to the regiment, and to the friends of those who are dead, reminding them of the scenes through which they have passed. An account is also given of the many hard fought battles in which the regiment participated, with a record of the officers and an alphabetical roster of the privates. Every member of the regiment may well feel proud that his fortunes were cast with such a noble band of our country's defenders.

RANDOM SKETCHES

AND

WANDERING THOUGHTS.

1862.

"They never fail who die
In a great Cause; the block may soak their gore,
Their heads may sodden in the sun; their limbs
Be strung to city gates or castle walls;
But still their spirits walk abroad, though years
Elapse, and others share as dark a doom,
They but augment the deep and sweeping thoughts
Which overspread all others, and conduct
The World at last to Freedom."

PATRIOTISM is one of the highest aspirations of the soul. In a country like ours, there is every possible inducement to give it the highest and purest expression. If the Laplander, chilling among his banks of snow—the Russian, ground by the heel of oppression—the Turk, forced to be the tool of power, lust and caprice—and the Chinaman, shut out from the world, where ignorant hordes are born and die, in their abjectness and poverty—if all these can bravely fight and die for their Country, what ought not the American citizen to feel and do in this great struggle for the preservation of Liberty and Self-Government?

At this moment a giant Rebellion is overshadowing our land, greater in magnitude than has ever been known in the World's history. Already has our fertile soil been deluged with the blood of her sons, who have gone forth in her defence. Many homes are already draped in mourning, their inmates weeping for loved ones slain. And mournful cries come wafting on every breeze from the Southern land, imploring help to put down treason, which seeks to destroy the Temple of Liberty erected by our Fathers.

In this great struggle for Freedom, there should be but one sentiment and one purpose—to save our Country with her free Constitutional rights unimpaired. And if that black stain upon our Nation's past record, Slavery, is blotted out in the conflict, let us all hail the day with supreme delight, and from its ruins build a more beautiful edifice, dedicated to Universal Freedom, whose broad dome may be as expansive as the blue vault of heaven above us, where myriads may continue to find a welcome home and shelter from the hand of tyranny and oppression.

It was in the summer of 1862 that I left the Barracks at Albany, having in charge one hundred and eighteen men, to join the Army of the Potomac. We took passage on the Steamer New World, and had a delightful trip on the silvery waters of the noble Hudson, beneath the calm rays of a harvest moon, which lit us on our way.

As early dawn broke in upon us, we found our boat nearing the wharf at New York. At roll call, all except two of the men answered to their names. A search was made for the absentees, and they were found secreted in the hold of the vessel—an initiatory step for desertion, which had become so common in our army. They were soon brought forth, and handcuffed for the balance of the journey.

Before crossing the river for Jersey City, I experienced much difficulty in keeping the men in the ranks, owing to their many pretended wants, most of them having some plausible desire to be gratified; but I remained firm in my purpose, not allowing any of them to leave, on any pretence whatever, until we arrived at the depot. Here I secured a large room, well adapted for my command, as many of them were deserters.

Having securely guarded the doors, with sentinels, I returned to New York, and spent the balance of the day in making purchases for my anticipated wants in the field.

After having secured my camp outfit, I rejoined my command at Jersey City and obtained transportation to convey them to Baltimore, arriving there the following day. I reported immediately to the Chief Quartermaster, who forwarded the men to their respective regiments, relieving me of my first command of Union soldiers.

It was in the streets of this city that the first blood was shed in defence of the Union, on that memorable day, the Seventeenth of April—the same month, and day of the month, that the first blood was shed in the Revolution of 1776, at Lexington, which is a singular coincidence; also, that the martyrs were from the same State.

From that day my heart beat high and warm. I felt the safety of our Republic, though my eyelids had often moistened when the ranks marched proudly by me, as I saw them from my window, on their way to the Capital, for its defence. Then mothers, maids and old men waved their handkerchiefs, that were wet with tears of their proud affection, and to-day I feel hopeful, although in the midnight of our cause, that victory will crown our banners.

On the arrival of my horses from New York, I left Baltimore for Washington, sending the horses by the overland route, a distance of forty miles, where I found them the next morning, in good condition.

Washington is a city of distances, laid out in wide avenues, of which Pennsylvania is the grandest, from which can be seen our splendid Capitol, with its magnificent dome towering to the sky, its base supported by most beautiful colonnades, wrought in most elaborate style; away to the west is seen the President's mansion, known as the White House, with its extensive grounds and pleasant walks. I visited the east room. It is painted and furnished in the most costly manner. Off to the right is seen Washington Monument, towering to the sky, like a huge pyramid, yet incomplete, the Treasury Building, Patent Office, and Post Office, are pure classical architecture, and are monuments of architectural skill and beauty.

I found Washington full of life, with regiment after regiment arriving from the loyal States, to help repel General Lee and "Stonewall" Jackson from invading

the Capital of the Nation.   The day after my arrival
I heard the first booming of cannon, far in the distance,
and saw the retreating Army of the Potomac again in
the field before Washington, ready to meet the rebel
hosts, who were so eager to pillage the council halls of
our Nation.

The first news we received was that General Pope
had been driven across the Rappahannock, and was
flying for safety to the defences of Washington.   The
Army of the Potomac was already on the march, and
hastening to his relief.   At this time a part of the rebel
army had crossed into Maryland.

The city was filled with excitement, and all means
of transportation pressed into service to convey the sick
and wounded from the battle fields.   The clerks of the
Departments were ordered to report at the Treasury
Building for duty, to assist in burying the dead and
relieving the wants of the wounded and dying soldiers.

On the 30th of August I reported for duty to Major
General Wadsworth, and was ordered to join my regiment at Yorktown.   The brigade to which they were
attached had been left to defend that place.   I took the
steamer for Alexandria, and on arriving there, found
all bustle and confusion.   The streets were filled with

mud. Troops were disembarking from transports, and moving forward toward the battle field of Bull Run. The second battle was then being fought; the artillery firing I distinctly heard.

While here, I visited the Marshall House, and saw the spot where Colonel Ellsworth fell, while in the act of hauling down the rebel flag which was floating over the building, and had been nailed there by the hands of its occupant. For that accursed emblem of treason, young Ellworth lost his life, and the traitor Jackson fell by the swift avenging hand of Frank Brownell. This was the only place of note I saw while at Alexandria.

The city presents a very unseemly appearance. The buildings are mostly old and dilapidated; the sidewalks were all mud; the courtyards and gardens were used for pig stys, cattle pens and correls. Such a sight, to a Northern man, was really offensive, I was glad to get on board a transport, which conveyed me to Old Point Comfort.

On our way thither, we passed the TOMB OF WASHINGTON, nearly hemmed in by the foliage growing on the banks of the river. There, in that quiet vault, lay the Patriot and Sage, the revered Father of his Country. Here, amid the quiet of country life, had he slumbered for more than half a century undisturbed, with the silent waters of the Potomac gliding just beneath his feet, and almost on the very spot where he spent his childhood's years. But how changed the scene! Now war is in the land, and traitors to the Government which he had helped to establish, through years of bloodshed and suffering, were in possession of this very soil, and threatened to disturb his last resting place. Our boat was gliding swiftly by, and I gazed on that sacred spot until MOUNT VERNON'S shades faded from my view. The memory of that hour will never be blotted out.

The Potomac is a beautiful river, rising among the Alleganies and winding down through Virginia and Maryland, until it empties into the Chesapeake Bay, at Point Lookout.

Here we left the land in the distance, and put out amid the breakers of the Chesapeake. The waters were quite rough, which tossed the vessel to and fro, and made me sick, compelling me to take a berth for the remainder of the trip.

On my arrival at Old Point, I found an immense quantity of shipping in the bay. Off to the right lay Hampton Roads, where the naval battle was fought between our fleet and the rebels, and where that terrible combat took place between the little Monitor and the huge Merrimac, in which the latter was driven to more quiet waters, only to meet destruction by its own hand. Off to the left lay the Rip Raps, where the chain gangs are made to work the balance of their enlistments, on the fortifications of Fort Wool. Farther beyond is seen Sewell's Point, and away off, near the horizon, lay Cape Henry, with its lighthouse, which tells the mariner the dangers he is likely to meet with, as he approaches the outlet to this great harbor.

I visited Fortress Monroe, and found fortifications of immense dimensions, sufficient to garrison fifteen thousand men, and mounted with guns of the largest calibre. Not far from me lay the Union and Lincoln guns, which are said to carry balls weighing four hundred and fifty pounds, and which require eighty pounds of powder to throw them a distance of six miles. This kind of arbitrament will no doubt prove the final Peacemaker between the North and South.

The Fortress is built of masonry and earthwork, its slopes, ramps and glacis, are neatly sodded, presenting a beautiful velvety appearance, of green color, bordered in blue, which effect the stone coping presents to the eye, at a short distance.

A deep moat surrounds the fortress, which is connected with the main land by drawbridges. The interior has casemates, caponniers, storerooms, offices and officers' quarters, all neatly fitted up for the purposes intended. The Parade is sodded, having wide graveled avenues running in every direction. This is the largest and best arranged fort we have in this country, and at present is the headquarters of Major General John A. Dix, one of the staunchest Union men in the country.

Old Point Comfort was once a place of great resort during the summer months, as a watering place for the Southern aristocracy. A little way up the James river is seen Newport News and Hampton, which latter place was burned by the rebels, at night, on the approach of our troops.

I took the steamer Thomas L. Morgan for Yorktown, late in the afternoon, and after a journey of three hours, arrived at the wharf. When I landed it was dark; lowering clouds were gathering in the western sky, and I felt a great desire to find shelter from the impending storm. A contraband kindly offered to guide me to our camp, for which I thanked him and accepted his services. We ascended the steep bluffs and traveled about half a mile through the winding fortification, which surrounds the place, to the south gate of the fort, which we passed, the countersign not being demanded from us by the sentinel.

I found my regiment encamped near by. The camp fires were blazing, and the boys seemed quite cheerful, living in this rude state, it being the first camp in which the regiment had been left long enough to cook a ration properly for five months; having passed this place after its seige, some two months previous, on their way to Richmond from Fortress Monroe, traveling night and day, through burning sun, fighting from Yorktown to Williamsburgh, Seven Pines, White Oak Swamp, and Malvern Hill, retreating to Harrison's Landing, and thence back to Yorktown.

One may readily imagine their condition. They were mostly without tents and clothing, with only such covering as their ingenuity could devise. The regiment had left home with ten hundred and forty men, all fit for duty. Now it could only muster about four hundred.

In this plight I found the regiment to which my fortunes were united.

Soon after my arrival, an attack was made on our outposts, by the enemy, and we were ordered within the fort. We pitched our tents on a high bluff, directly above York river, which gave us a most beautiful view of the bay in the distance,· and of Gloucester Point.

These fortifications are immense, covering an area of some four hundred acres, including the village of Yorktown and the old fortifications built in 1787, which are yet visible.

There is an old graveyard in the village, situated on one of the bluffs of York river, whose tombstones will carry you back to the sixteenth century, on whose tablets are engraven the names of Nelson, Fairfax, and other old Virginian families of note.

Near by is the old mansion of Governor Nelson, which was occupied by Lord Cornwallis, as his headquaters, during the seige of Yorktown, in 1783. In the south gable are distinctly visible cannon shots which were sent from our artillery, by order of the Governor himself, and which drove the occupants from the building. It is now used as a hospital for our sick and wounded soldiers.

The bricks which were used in constructing this building were imported from England. The porch, which stood in front, has been torn away; the garden wall has crumbled down, and in its stead a hedge fence is seen, formed of box, which grows luxuriant in this climate, and is found in abundance here.

Like most other mansions in the South, it is neglected and going fast into decay. A few years hence, scarcely a landmark will be left of the old Cavaliers who once prided themselves on their homes and ancestry.

York river is noted for the depth of its channel and its fine fish and oysters. The scenery around is rather monotonous. One vast field of pine forest carries the eye to its utmost scope, in which the sun apparently sets, and the echo of the evening gun dies amid its foliage.

To-day is muster-day. The boys are in fine spirits, but longing for the Paymaster, whom they have not seen for the last six months. Many of them are penni-less. But no doubt the Government is doing the best it can at present, and will soon be able to meet their wants. In the meantime, great inconvenience is expe-rienced by many, and several amusing as well as serious complaints were made by the men to their officers. One day a private came to his captain with a very long face, saying that he had just received a letter from his wife, in which she stated that the pork barrel was empty, and the flour almost gone, and if he did not soon send home money she would have to make other arrangements The poor fellow, with tears in his eyes, said: "Captain, how would you feel if your wife should write to you that she would have to make 'other arrangements'?" •

This afternoon I took a ride on horseback along the banks of the York river. After riding about three miles, I came to a by-path leading off into the woods, and gave a loose rein to the animal; he followed it a distance of three miles. It led into an open field, through which there was a road. I followed the road a short way, which brought me in sight of an old mansion, whose gray boards and fallen verandah roof told plainly that time was making its impression. I spurred my horse and galloped on, and soon reached the "Plantation Home." The girls who stood at the door and saw my approach, ran up stairs. The proprietor met me at the gate and invited me in, which invitation I accepted, and spent nearly an hour in conversation with the old gentleman, but no women made their appearance. I learned by the conversation I had with him that they favored the Confederacy, and were strong believers in State Rights.

I began to fear that there might be some plan laid for my capture, and not feeling inclined to visit Richmond as a prisoner of war, concluded to leave, excusing myself on account of its being so late in the afternoon. The sun had just set, and I was five miles from camp, and beyond our lines, away from any other habitation. I mounted my horse and galloped away. The moon was just peeping up from the eastern sky, throwing her mellow light on field and forest. I reached the wood-path I had lately left and traveled quietly along through the swamp and chaparral, which somewhat impeded my advance, all the while keeping a sharp lookout for bushwhackers, who infest the surrounding country.

I suddenly came to a halt, finding an impassable barrier before me, consisting of slashings. My first thoughts were to bivouac for the night, but finally concluded to make camp that night, at all hazard. After traveling for an hour through the dense forest, I found a road which brought me out near Fort Magruder, and within two miles of our camp, which I saw lighted up in the distance.

On my way thither, I passed the spot on which Lord Cornwallis surrendered his sword, in 1783. This memorable spot is enclosed with a neat cedar fence, containing an area of about thirty feet square. Here occurred the closing scene of the American Revolution, the surrender of the last British Army on our soil.

Adjoining this little enclosure is one still dearer to every lover of his country—THE UNION SOLDIER's BURIAL GROUND, which is laid out in avenues, and enclosed with a Virginia rail fence; each grave having a headboard, neatly marked, telling the hero's name, his company and regiment. In this sacred enclosure lies interred those who have sacrificed their lives on their country's altar, for the cause of Liberty. In this lonely resting place on the plains of Yorktown, sleeps many a noble boy, far from his home and kindred, with no kind friend to drop a tear, or sing a funeral requiem.

I visited this spot by pale moonlight, when all was quiet. Such feelings as then filled my breast can never again be realized, for they come but once in a lifetime.

I arrived in camp late in the evening and soon found repose on my rustic couch, falling into a quiet slumber, only to be awakened by an alarm that our pickets had been driven in at Williamsburgh, with a cry of "To arms! to arms!" from the shrill bugle.

The thoughts of the late battle are still fresh in our minds, and again the alarm is given, all expecting the same scenes to be re-enacted. The battle of Williamsburgh was the first field of blood our regiment had witnessed.

"I could imagine," said a friend of mine, who was on the field of battle, and wandered over it, "nothing more terrible than the silent indications of agony that marked the features of the pale corpses which lay at every step. Though dead and rigid in every muscle, they still writhed and seemed to turn to catch the passing breeze for a cooling breath; staring eyes, gaping mouths, clenched hands and strangely contracted limbs, seemingly drawn into the smallest compass, as if by a mighty effort to rend asunder some irresistible bond which held them down to the torture of which they died. One sat against a tree, and with mouth and eyes open, looked up into the sky, as if to catch a glance at its fleeting spirit. Another had grasped his faithful musket, and the compression of his mouth told of determination which would have been fatal to a foe, had life ebbed a moment later. A third clung with both hands to a bayonet which was buried in the ground. Near by lay a rebel Major, who had been in deadly conflict with five Union soldiers. His countenance told the terrible conflict he had just encountered. The dead almost covered the field. The wood near by had been set on fire by the retreating foe, for the purpose of burning the dead who had fallen there. The stench was almost impossible to endure by our advancing column."

The Union troops had fought on this field with a steadiness and determination rarely witnessed, and this exhibition of their courage taught a lesson to Southern rebels, of a spirit that they had not expected in an enemy whose valor they had been accustomed to deride and sneer at, since the commmencement of Yankee aggression, as they termed it.

November has arrived, bringing no chilly winds nor frosty nights. The air is balmy, and the wild flowers are yet in bloom. From my quarters I can see the boys bathing in the river; also, with their feet, digging up clams, which are found here in great abundance.

Last night I was awakened from my dreams by music. The moon was shining brightly, throwing her mild rays over our camp. I arose and went to my tent door, from which I saw a figure robed in white, standing in the centre of one of our camp streets, apparently singing to the moon. The song was a great favorite in camp. The chorus runs thus:

> " Roll on, silver Moon, guide the traveler his way,
>   While the nightingale's song is in tune;
> I 'll never, never more, with my true lover stray,
>   By the sweet silver light of the Moon."

A crowd soon gathered around him, dressed in the robes of night, presenting a very comical appearance.

The officer of the day was making his grand rounds; on his arrival, he ordered the men to their quarters, and reprimanded the gay Lieutenant for molesting the camp after "taps."

I have just recovered from a severe attack of camp fever, caused by the want of proper diet, which we have not been able to obtain for the last three months.

Thanksgiving has brought us a feast of fat things. Through the exertions of our surgeons a table was spread beneath the grateful covering of two large tents, the mild autumnal weather allowing the entrance to them to be opened; the Southern breeze imparting more of a genial temperature to the interior, than otherwise. After a blessing by the Chaplain, the guests drew around the sumptuous board, and indulged in a splendid dinner, such as had not satiated the appetite of any soldier before, during the Peninsular campaign.

This little gathering of friends who are all embarked in one common cause, assembling to commemorate the day of general thanksgiving throughout the North, was marked by universal hilarity, good feeling, and sentiments abounding in wit, from the fluent tongues of the officers. "The Red, White and Blue" was sung in fine style, by one of the guests, and the ancient and humorous song of the "Hobbies," by the same, the chorus by the entire party. "The Sword of Bunker Hill" was also beautifully executed; all of which added greatly to the festivities of the day. An aged Captain entertained us with two original stories, in which it was easy to perceive "where the laugh came in."

The toasts finished the programme of the day. The first was given by our Colonel: "The Commander-in-Chief of the Army and Navy, of this our once happy but now distracted country, 'Honest Old Abe.' Let us each stand by him as long as we have a pulse that can beat, or a drop of blood that can be spilt." This was received with demonstrations of applause, and was as appropriate as patriotic.

The Colonel is laboring under great physical disability, occasioned by his wounds, and the closing sentence of his toast, uttered beneath the tattered colors of the regiment, which he led to that memorable battle field, was nearly verified in his person.

The Chaplain offered the following: "Our Friends at Home" Responded to by our Surgeon in a humorous and happy style, in which he said: "On this occasion, as well as many others during the past few months, we have adopted, from necessity, the French motto, 'When one has not that which he likes, he must like that which he has,' but my friend's allusion to home reminds us it cannot always serve, so: 'Here's to the gal I left behind me.'" This was received with applause, each one sharing with the Surgeon, from feelings of personal sympathy, the sentiments embodied in his toast.

The Assistant Surgeon proposed the following: "Our Colonel—may he be speedily restored to health, and return to duty among us." A hearty endorsement of this expression was evinced in the approbation with which it was received.

The following was also given: "Surgeons, present and absent; may they never stand in need of our services—nor we of theirs."

A hearty approval of the two concluding toasts was manifested, and with expressions of thanks to the gentlemen for their kindness and hospitality, we withdrew, just as the echoes of the sunset gun were dying away in the pine forests.

The next day I rode out on horseback to survey the earthworks thrown up by General McClellan, during his advance on Yorktown. They were many miles in length, and quite formidable. I also passed through the pond, on horseback, where the Fifth regiment of Green Mountain boys made their desperate charge on the rebel works. Near by stood an Observatory, built during the seige, in log house style, with

ladder to ascend from the outside. This towered up
above the tallest trees, from whose top could be viewed
the enemy's movements. On my return to camp, my
horse fell, throwing me headlong on the ground, laying
me by his side, "Like a warrior taking his rest." We
both arose at once. I mounted him and rode to camp,
feeling somewhat damaged.

For the last three weeks our boys have been building winter quarters, which the chilly winds and snows
of December admonish them to do. They have just
completed them, and to-night we received orders to
be ready to embark on board of transports for some
unknown point. The camp is all tumult and confusion. The men threatening to destroy their work,
compelling the officers to use severe measures to quell
insubordination.

We are relieved by a brigade of drafted men from
Pennsylvania. Many of them are substitutes, and have
been paid as high as a thousand dollars by the principal. My opinion is, that they will not make the soldiers our volunteers do. A man who leaves his home,
wife and little ones, and all that is dear to him, is
inspired with different feelings and motives from those
who are bought or forced to fight. A regiment of the
latter is worth a brigade of the former. However,

this is an experiment of the Government, and time will show whether my views are correct or not. I like the voluntering system, for on that strong arm must our Government depend for the maintenance of her honor and the perpetuity of her free institutions.

Our transports sailed southward, stopping at Fortress Monroe, where we were transferred to other vessels suitable for sea. We set sail with sealed orders. Off Cape Henry they were to be opened. As we passed out to sea the wind freshened somewhat, but the sun went down in glorious clouds of purple and crimson, and the evening was fair and calm above us. During the night we passed Cape Henry, and morning dawn found us on the broad ocean, the land only a blue line in the distance. A few hours and that disappeared.

The next morning I was on deck, watching the gradual rising of the sun in the distant waters. The day passed quietly; some reading, some speculating on the probable results of the war, while others were lying sick below, in their berths, and some casting up their *accounts* over the bulwarks of the vessel, noting the shifting hues and forms of the waves, as the fish swallowed the contents of their stomachs. As the afternoon advanced, the clouds began to gather, and the distant roll of thunder told us a storm was fast approaching. The sun was hid from our sight, and soon the dark mantle of night covered the mighty deep. Naught was heard except the dull roar of the ocean, and the roll of the distant thunder. The white-crested waves began to look like sheets of fire, as they rolled mountains high. A more sublime sight my eyes never beheld. No pen can portray the grandeur of the ocean in a storm.

1863.

IT is New Year's morning, and our vessel is in sight of Fort Macon, where can be seen the Stars and Stripes floating from her ramparts. They were hailed with three cheers by all on board, and a welcome to our destined port, which was Beaufort, North Carolina.

Our vessel soon reached the wharf, and landed our regiment once more on terra firma, six hundred strong. We took up our line of march for Carolina City, where we encamped in shelter tents, which each man carried with him as a part of his baggage. On reaching the city, which consisted of four houses, one corn crib, two barns, a small railroad depot, and a few fishermen's huts, we pitched our tents, stowed ourselves away for the night, and dreamed of the festivities of home, and the little ones there. The heavy march of that day will be long remembered by us all. The weather, for this season of the year, was very pleasant during the day, although the nights were quite cool. Having no fire, and sleeping on the cold earth, made it rather disagreeable for those who had enjoyed better quarters.

While we lay at this place awaiting further orders, the following complimentary address was issued to our brigade by the General commanding:

"The General lately commanding the brigade most happily takes this occasion to congratulate the officers and soldiers with whom he has been so intimately associated.

"While memory lasts, it will continually recur to the scenes of deprivation, danger, blood and battle, through which you have passed, and you will remember your inexperience and discontent, and then your discipline and friendly, happy affiliation.

"All will remember with regret the deadly effects of the swamps before Yorktown.

"You were the first in advance upon Williamsburgh, and when ordered by General McClellan to support General Hancock, the enemy gave up the contest.

"On the 19th of May, at Bottoms Bridge, you waded waist deep in the swamps of the Chickahominy, you drove away the enemy, and were the first to cross that stream.

"On the 23d, one hundred and seventy of your number made a reconnoissance from Bottoms Bridge to the James river, near Drury's Bluff, and returned, bringing valuable information.

"On the 24th, 25th and 26th, after other troops had failed, you made the gallant, dashing reconnoissance of the Seven Pines, driving the superior force of General Stewart from Bottoms Bridge to within four miles of Richmond, the position nearest that city ever occupied by our troops.

"On the 31st of May, at Fair Oaks, or Seven Pines, occupying the above advance position, your brigade made the most desperate, bloody and obstinate fight of the war, and while we mourn the loss of one-half of our comrades in arms, you have the consolation of knowing that by your heroic sacrifice and stubborn resistance you saved the Army of the Potomac from great disaster.

"On the 27th, 28th and 29th of June, the rebel General Jackson hurled his immense force upon our right, and passed that flank of the army, and turned with extreme solicitude towards the rear at Bottoms Bridge, which, if crossed, would result in irretreivable ruin; and it should be a source of great pride and satisfaction in the future to remember that all this intense anxiety was dispelled, and all breathed with relief and felt secure, when it rapidly ran through the army that Naglee's Brigade had destroyed the bridge, and stood night and day, for three days, in the middle of the Chickahominy, successfully and continually resisting its passage.

"Again, on the following day, you held a post of the greatest importance and danger. At the White Oak Swamp the most determined efforts of the enemy to cross the bridge in pursuit of our army were thwarted by our artillery, and you stood for ten hours supporting it, quiet spectators of the most terrific cannonade, while other regiments were only kept in place by being ordered back when they approached your lines. Retreating all night, you stood ready in position on the following day, expecting to be ordered to take part in the battle of Malvern Hill.

"Retreating again all night, at Carter's Hill, on the second of July, you stood by the artillery and wagon train, and, when all expected it would be destroyed, you brought it safely to Harrison Landing.

"During December, you destroyed a dozen large salt works in Mathews county, Virginia, and drove the Rangers from that county, as well as from Gloucester, Middlesex and King and Queens counties;

captured large herds, intended for the rebel army, and destroyed all their barracks, stables and stores.

"At Yorktown, from August to the end of December, you have restored the works at that place and Gloucester Point, and they are by your labor rendered strong and defensible.

"Thus is yours the honor of being the first to pass, and the last to leave, the Chickahominy; and while you lead the advance from this memorable place to near Richmond, you were last in the retreating column, when, after seven days of constant fighting, it reached a place of security and rest at Harrison Landing.

"Your decendants for generations will boast of the gallant conduct of the regiments to which you belong, and when all are laid in the dust, History will still proclaim the glorious deeds performed by you.

"Go on. 'Truth is mighty and will prevail.' Pretenders for a time may rob you of your just deserts, but, as you have experienced, their evil reports will certainly be exposed—for your many friends at home, ever watchful of and identified with your reputation, will see that justice will be done.

"A new page in your history is about to be written. Let it be still more brilliant than that already known. Your past good conduct has won the warmest esteem and confidence of your late brigade commander. He has no apprehensions for the future."

We were again ordered on board of transports, which lay in the bay, near Fort Macon. At sundown we got on board, amidst a heavy, rolling sea, tossing our vessel to and fro, which told plainly.Old Neptune was angry.

After much delay we joined the expedition, which consisted of fifty vessels, all under, the command of Major General Foster. We weighed anchor and set sail southward, under sealed orders. When off Wilmington they were opened, and we found our destination to be Port Royal, South Carolina. The sea continued rough, causing much sickness on board.

After a sail of forty-eight hours, we anchored in Port Royal bay. This Department is commanded by Major General Hunter. A misunderstanding occurred between the two Generals. This unhappy difficulty delayed the purposes of the expedition, and for some days the troops were compelled to remain on board the transports, much against their wishes. The difficulty was finally adjusted; and, after running up to Beaufort, South Carolina, we returned and landed the troops on St. Helena Island.

After the troops had disembarked, we commenced unloading the stock, which is rather a strange sight to a landsman. The cattle are driven through the gangway of the vessel into the sea, the water being too shallow for the vessel to reach the shore, which made it necessary to anchor in the stream. They were headed toward the shore, by some of the crew, in boats. They are all natural swimmers, and soon found safety on shore. In this way many thousands can be unloaded in a very short time, and very seldom are any lost.

The horses were taken from the hold of the vessel by means of a sling made of sackcloth and ropes, which is put under them, passing over their backs, to which a block and tackle is attached; they are then hoisted to the main deck and swung over the side of the vessel, by means of a yard arm, and let down into the sea, where they are detached from the sling and readily swim to shore.

It is quite surprising to see these poor animals yield so readily when once off their feet, hanging in mid air. Many of them were terribly bruized, and had suffered much during the voyage, as they will never lay down to rest while on shipboard; their first desire, on reaching land, is to do so, that they may rest their swollen limbs, which is to them a greater luxury than feed.

4

St Helena island is one of the most beautiful of the Sea Islands, and is noted for producing the finest cotton in the world. There is also grown here large quantities of lemons and oranges. I visited a grove some four miles from our camp, consisting of several acres of trees, from which I cut some walking sticks. There is an old dilapidated mansion here, the owners having abandoned it, and, I was informed, had joined the rebel army, and their negroes had fled to our lines for safety and protection.

This old mansion bears the marks of time. Everything appeared to be going to waste. It no doubt was a heritage bequeathed to a prodigal son, they being so common in the South.

A large number of acres on this plantation were fitted for the cultivation of rice, on land situated for overflow of water, which rice requires at certain stages of its growth. The building is used as a signal station by our Corps, this point being nearly midway from Hilton Head to Beaufort.

St. Helena Island is some sixteen miles long and extends from Beaufort to the ocean, which point is termed Landsend. On this point is situated Fort Beauregard, captured by our navy.

I visited Beaufort, which lies fourteen miles from Hilton head, on an island of that name. This was once the most aristocratic place in the South. Our forces found it entirely abandoned on their arrival here, with the exception of one man, and he was too drunk to get away. The inhabitants, in their flight, left all except such things as they could carry with them and make good their escape. Many of them were made to believe the Union troops were Vandals, who only came for the purpose of ravishing their women, capturing their negroes, carrying them to Cuba, for the purpose of selling them, the proceeds of which sales were to help pay the expenses of the war. Many of the negroes have returned and are now occupying the dwellings of their former masters, and enjoying the privilege of using a walking stick, and smoking a cigar, which was considered an offence before the Union army came. Such was Southern liberty.

At this place I found a regiment of Southern troops (colored), called the First South Carolina Volunteers, all well armed and equipped, and they compare well with any troops in the service, that I have seen. Their courage and fighting qualities I cannot doubt—for they love liberty, and hate slavery, and are willing to fight for their freedom.

Beaufort is pleasantly situated and handsomely built, having many fine architectural productions. Its streets are wide, and well shaded with trees. Most of the houses have gardens, which are beautifully laid out, studded with shrubbery of all kinds, suitable for the climate, and for all seasons of the year. Fruit is grown in large abundance here, such as peaches, pears, figs, lemons, oranges and pomegranates. The trees are now in full blow, delighting the eye of the beholder with their scarlet blossoms.

On the main street, facing the bay, stands the house in which the first Secesh meeting was held, the residence of Barnwell Rhett, a notorious South Carolina nullifier and traitor of the Calhoun school.

As I stood under the shade of a magnificent tree, gazing intently into the garden which surrounded the mansion, I drank in the quiet spirit of the scene. I thought how base a use this noble mansion had subserved. Beneath that very roof and these garden walks, with its budding orange groves and twining myrtles, but one year ago sat the leading traitors of our country, deliberately planning, in sober council, the ruin of our Government. Here, on this very spot, was nursed and matured this gigantic rebellion, which has made so many widows and fatherless children, that ambitious slave owners might have their fling at the best Government in the world, and on its ruins establish one instead, devoted to Slavery and Free Trade.

Near by stands the house in which our own starry-eyed Mitchell died, of that dreadful disease, yellow fever. The history of both these houses are significant, and will never be forgotton. Off to the right is a quiet nook in the bay, near which stands the fine old mansion of Robert Barnwell, who was an advocate of State Rights and Secession, and is now a representative in the so-called Confederate Congress at Richmond.

This house bears the marks of time. Its antique architecture, its rotten columns, decayed verandah floors, weather beaten sheathing and moss covered roof, all tell that a century has elapsed since its erection. This house is now occupied by a widow lady and her two daughters, whose charms make it a resort for many of our officers. They are from Boston, and came out here for the purpose of teaching the blacks, and belonged to what was called "Gideon's Band," a set of fanatics who thought the negro a little better than the white man. They finally abandoned the Sisterhood and opened an officers' boarding house, which they found far more profitable and congenial to their taste.

During my stay here, I received an invitation to attend a marriage ceremony, which took place at the Episcopal church, in the evening. General Saxton was the recipient of the hand of a Miss Thompson, formerly of the band, and was a teacher on one of the plantations. The groom was dressed in full military uniform; the bride in pure white, with a wreath of flowers, fresh from the garden, around her head. The altar and pulpit of the church were decorated most beautifully with flowers and evergreens, whose perfumes filled the house with delicious odor. This was in early spring time, and produced a most charming effect on the senses. My visit to Beaufort was pleasant, and I shall long remember the widow and her charming daughters.

On my return, I stopped at Paris Island. Near the landing stands a low roofed veranded house, which is so common in the South, but a few steps from where the surf beats against the shore. It stands in a wilderness of roses, orange trees and tall oleanders, whose fragrance filled the air, and was scattered far around by the sea breeze, to many a quiet nook.

A camp lay in the distance, each tent looking like a monument erected to the dead, and all was so quiet, cool and shady, accompanied with the constant murmur of the ocean, fills the air with so pleasant a dreaminess that I thought that hither one might come weary of the busy world and live contented forever.

A little farther down is seen Hilton Head, with her hundred of masts peering up from the ocean, and the black smoke stacks of the monstrous ocean steamers and those of the little monitors, sending up fire and smoke, as if Vulcan had his forge beneath the briny deep, and was determined to make us smell a sulphurous pit before our time.

The Arago had just arrived at Hilton Head, from the North, loaded with a thousand different articles to supply the wants of the soldiers. A great crowd gathered around the Express and Postoffice, each one eager to receive his packages and letters first from the office of distribution.

The whistle blew and the bell rang, followed by a shout, "All on board!" which brought the passengers, and the Planter, with her black pilot, Robert Small, left for St. Helena Island. This was the same craft that left Charleston by the inland waters, and came to Beaufort unmolested, much to the astonishment of the natives and officer in command at that place. The last dying rays of a Southern sunset had disappeared, when the black Captain landed me at St. Helena. I reached

camp just as the echos of the evening gun were dying on
the distant waters.   The inspirational feelings a sunset
produces here cannot be described by tongue nor pen.

To-day our regiment was inspected, after which
they formed a hollow square, and from the center was
read the following patriotic resolutions, which were
unanimously adopted by the regiment:

"The officers and soldiers of the Eighty-first Regiment New York Volunteers, citizens of the State of
New York, having no recent opportunity of joining
their voices with those of her loyal citizens at home,
deem it proper in this manner to express their views
and sentiments in regard to events and measures now
absorbing the attention of the country, to the end that
our friends at the North may strengthen their faith in
our cause and increase their zeal for the suppression
of the rebellion against which we fight; therefore,

"*Resolved,* That our Government, which started
with principles declared, objects and aims set forth,
that must challenge the admiration of mankind, and
that cost as much of patriot blood and treasure, hard-
ship and privation, as was required to maintain and
prosecute seven years war with one of the most powerful nations of the world, is now worth as firm pledges

and determined support as at the beginning of its existence, and that it may justly demand and exact them of its citizens; therefore, we hail with joy the recent action of Congress, placing in the hands of the President power and means adequate for such purpose.

"*Resolved*, That, while white men are liable to conscription, and their property to appropriation, there can be no valid reason why 'other persons,' whose rights above all others, have become involved in the issue of this contest, should be exempted or prohibited from giving such aid and support to our cause as they may give, and that whenever and wherever a colored man may become available in suppressing the rebellion, then and there his services should be required.

"*Resolved*, That when we enlisted in our country's service, we put aside all political differences, and left our homes to sustain her flag, maintain its glory and fame, and rather than see one star stricken from its azure field, or one stripe torn from its borders, we would see every rod of territory in which this viper, Rebellion, nests, a desolate waste of savage wilderness; sooner than consent to a peace that shall tarnish its glory, or sully its fame, we would lay our bones to bleach beside the graves of our fallen comrades, upon soil already hallowed by their blood.

" *Resolved,* That if the time comes when our country requires that our thinned ranks be filled, and her strength be replenished, we will look for prompt and cheerful acquiescence at home, and able and substantial men to help us; and if at home any remain whose cowardice conquers their patriotism, or whose mercenary love of gold exceeds their love of their country's honor, we leave them to the scorn and indignation of our mothers, wives and sisters, whose prayers and hands are ever raised to sustain and comfort us here."

A grand review of all the troops on the island came off to-day. They were reviewed by Major General Hunter and staff. We were also favored with the presence of his lady, which was quite a curiosity to many soldiers, as some had not seen a lady for months, and it was really refreshing, like an oasis in the desert to the weary traveler.

The troops numbered about 15,000, and were complimented by the General for their soldierly appearance and discipline. He also complimented our regiment for their taste and love of the beautiful, as displayed by our men in decorating their quarters and grounds, which was mostly done with palm and palmetto trees, and presented a very pretty appearance.

On the fifth of April, eighteen hundred and sixty-three, all the troops embarked on board of transports for Charleston, South Carolina. Our regiment was assigned to the steamship City of Bath. During the night the troops were got on board, and at daybreak we were ready to sail.

The morning is beautiful and clear The God of day has just arisen from his repose. A fine breeze is blowing from the west, all anchors are raised, and the entire division is moving toward that hotbed of treason, Charleston. The first division left during the night, accompanied by General Hunter and staff. The day was pleasant, and it being Sunday, our Chaplain preached from the hurricane deck. He gave us a fine discourse, forcibly impressing on the minds of the soldiers their duty to their God and their country.

About 5 o'clock we anchored at the mouth of the North Edisto river. We were piloted up the Edisto and anchored opposite a small village called Rockville, which is situated on a tributary of the Edisto. We lay here for five days, which time was mostly occupied in gathering shells on the beach, and oysters, which grow here in their natural state. There appeared acres of them when the tide was out, growing upright in clusters like grains of wheat in the head. Many of them are large, of fine flavor, and nearly as good as those cultivated at the North.

This morning a party of six, including myself, made a reconnoissance of Rockville. We went in a small boat. When we arrived within gunshot, I minutely examined the place with a field glass. No living thing could be discovered. All was quiet, and seemed entirely abandoned. We had been informed that a rebel regiment lay just in the rear of the village, in a thick wood, in which they were secreted. The next day our mortar boats sent over some shell, which no doubt disturbed them.

Our evenings have passed away quite pleasantly; each evening we have what is called a circus on board. The performance consisted of singing, dancing and recitations from *dramatic authors;* all of which were executed much to the credit of the artists. The audience room was the cabin in which we ate, slept, and performed. The real circus took place after tattoo, which consisted of grand and lofty tumbling by those who imbibed whisky too freely. The more sober ones laughed at their folly, and usually put the artists to bed about midnight, when peace and quiet was restored. The soldier's life has its bright side as well as its dark one.

Two days after our arrival at this place, at 4 o'clock in the afternoon, the first ball was fired from our ironclads at Fort Sumter. The firing continued from the ironclads and sand batteries along the shore until dark. The next day a council of war was held, which, after deliberation, concluded not to continue the assault.

On the tenth of April, at noon, our division was ordered back to Port Royal. We weighed anchor and the whole fleet set out for sea. In crossing the bar our vessel struck four times, and so hard as to throw her boilers out of place, which produced leakage. The pumps were set at work, and a flag of distress hoisted, which brought the Key West to our relief. She took us in tow, bringing us in safety to Hilton Head on the following morning.

Here we disembarked. It was near sundown before we took up our line of march for our camping ground, which lay about three miles out, and was beyond the fortifications. It was midnight when we arrived there with our camp equipage. We were all much fatigued, and bivouaced for the night, with the blue sky, filled with twinkling stars, for our covering. I soon fell into the arms of Morpheus, and was lost to all the hardships of war, and the pleasant memory of home, which so often cheers the weary and lonely hours, and makes life light and free from care.

Hilton Head is an island on which Port Royal postoffice is situated. It is one of the Sea Islands, and is chiefly used for the cultivation of cotton. On the northeast end is situated Fort Walker, which was taken at the same time Fort Beauregard surrendered.

The fortifications on this island are immense, occupying an area of some two hundred acres, which is mostly stockaded and deeply intrenched. The soil is a pale yellow sand, instead of a black mold, which I expected to find it, and which seemed useless for agricultural purposes, until I noticed it glistened with white particles, which I found to be pulverized shell. It is this that gives the soil its strength and sustenence.

The principal trees which grow here are the palmetto and live oak. The latter is a straggling grower, making an immense shade, for which purpose they are often times transplanted. At a distance they resemble our apple trees, both in foliage and form. The former grows upright, free from limbs a distance of ten and sometimes fifteen feet. At the top of the trunk their leaves spread out in great abundance, resembling an umbrella, making a beautiful shade for the negro driver to sit under, when the sun is too scorching to use the whip. These trees are interspersed all over the cotton fields, and I was informed that they were left for that purpose. The wood is porous, resembling cork, and is said to last longer in salt water than any other kind of timber.

In the tops of these trees, where the young leaves are found, grows a kind of cabbage, which is eaten by the negroes, and is said to very much resemble our cabbage in flavor.

Here, early in the month of March, I found flowers in full bloom, of almost every color, whose fragrance filled the air with perfume. The jasmin grows rankly in this loose sand, as well as the rose and honeysuckle. The orange trees were white with blossoms. The magnolia was just opening her spicy mouth, sending forth her delicious breath on the evening air.

Oh, how delightful it is to wander amid those groves by moonlight, and think of loved ones far away! In such hours as these memory brings to us our earliest and fondest associations, yet still I am discontented and sigh for something better than earth can give.

The landscape in this region of country is rather monotonous, its carriage drives miserable, and by-paths tedious. In my rambles now and then I found a

quiet nook, which speaks of a peace that the sur-
rounding·war has not yet succceded in disturbing.
All the day long the birds sing merrily, of which the
mocking bird is Queen, not in beauty but in song.
She sends forth her notes in all the varied tones.
Sometimes she has the hoarse caw of the crow, then
the mew of the cat, and then her own peculiarly sweet
voice. These little natives of the forest are so free
from want and care that man may really envy them
their happiness.

We lay at Hilton Head only two days, when we
received orders to proceed to Newbern, North Carolina,
for the purpose of reinforcing General Foster. The sky
began to darken, and the winds commenced blowing
a perfect gale, with heavy rain. The transports which
were to convey us to that place could not reach the
wharf, and were obliged to lay at anchor in the bay
until the storm subsided. Our quarters became flooded
with water, making them untenable, and myself and
tent-mate concluded to abandon them; so we started
through the rain for the beach, where the headquarters
of the brigade were established. It was very dark,
and we lost our direction, which, after an hour's travel,
brought us on the beach, about a mile above the point

we were trying to make, following the shore until we arrived at the camp, where we found good quarters for the night; but we were drenching wet, which made us feel rather uncomfortable.

That night, for the first time in my life, I slept on the ocean shore, and enjoyed its deep, sweet music. I felt that the Poet fully realized it all, when he said:

"There is a pleasure in the pathless woods;
  There is a rapture on the lonely shore;
  There is society where none intrudes,
    By the deep sea, and music in its roar,
  From this our interview, in which I steal
    From all I may be, or have been before,
  To mingle with the Universe, and feel
    What I can ne'er express, yet cannot all conceal."

Morning came with a cloudless sky. The sun came peeping up from his ocean bed, where he had slumbered for the night, and kissed the horizon with his effulgent rays, which betokened a pleasant day for our anticipated journey. We struck our tents, and took a double quick for the transport Belvidere, which lay waiting for us. The afternoon was far advanced when the troops and camp equipage was on board.

At sundown we passed over the bar, and was once more on the billows of the deep blue sea, and soon Port Royal lay far in the distance, appearing to us like a huge bank of sand. I took my blanket and lay down on the deck for the night, as berths could not be had. I found it quite wet and uncomfortable. We made good headway during the night and the following day, and at night anchored off Cape Lookout

Early the next morning we entered Old Topsail inlet, passed under the guns of Fort Macon, and landed at Morehead. From here we took the cars for Newbern, arriving there at sundown, and encamped along the Goldsboro Railroad, under the guns of Fort Rowan. During the night we received marching orders to move at daylight, with five days rations. Early dawn found our regiment ready for the march, and eager for the raid which had been promised them. But, to our great disappointment, the orders were countermanded. We remained here until the second day of May, when our regiment was ordered to Beaufort, Fort Macon and Morehead. Our headquarters were established at the latter place, on Calico creek.

This morning, May 18th, a party of fifty, myself being one of the number, started on a pony hunt, as it is called here, which was to take place about eighteen miles off, on Shackleford banks, which lay to the eastward. Pony penning was something new to us soldiers, and we were all excited for the sport.

We had chartered a small steamboat, and took in tow a flatboat and a small sail boat, which we understood would be necessary to land us on shore, as the water was very shallow at that point. The day was beautiful. The forest trees were dressed in their loveliest foliage, which is so pleasing to the eye after a cold, bleak winter. We sailed about fifteen miles in the steamer, when suddenly we ran aground, and found it impossible to proceed any further, as the tide was fast falling, so we got on board the flatboat, hoisted all sail and went three miles further, when we grounded with her. The only alternative left us was to jump overboard and wade to shore, or have the negroes carry us, who were anxiously waiting in the distance for a job. Some of the party brought them to their relief, but most of us concluded to take our own conveyance. When we arrived at the shore, we found a swamp, which we had to pass through for nearly a mile before we could reach dry land, and see the pony penning.

We were fast, and had to face the difficulty. The negroes led the way with their passengers on their backs, and we followed, going up to our knees in mud and water. It was a rather comical sight to see the negroes with men on their backs, larger than themselves, puffing and blowing as if ready to fall beneath their weight. Suddenly one of them fell, throwing his rider headlong into the mud. One grand hurrah went up from the crowd, and for a few moments was heard some tall swearing from the unfortunate rider, who accused the darkey of falling on purpose to amuse us footmen in the rear, for which he threatened to shoot him, in case of its recurrence. He mounted the negro again, pistol in hand, and off they went, the negro landing his rider in safety.

A short distance brought us to the pens. There we found a crowd of Secesh, some two hundred, mostly red haired, lantern-faced gentlemen. Many of the wild ponies had been caught and penned. The pens are yards enclosed with a rail fence some eight feet high. After they are secured in these yards, the negroes go in and capture such as they wish to brand, bringing them out and throwing them down, when the brand is applied to the fore shoulder, which has the marks of the owner on it. Such ponies as are not sold are again allowed to run at large. These ponies run wild and live in the marshes, on wild grass, digging their own wells for fresh water, with their feet. They grow from six to eight hands high. Some are finely formed, and, it is said, will endure much fatigue.

I soon became tired of pony penning, and took a stroll across the island, through the deep and burning sand. The sun was excessively hot, and I was glad to reach the beach, where I could lay down to rest. Here was a grand sight. The tide was coming in. The waves were tossing and rolling like boiling water; I saw a vessel in the distance, which seemed forcing its way through the mighty surges, as if seeking a safe harbor.

Immense numbers of sea gulls infest these shores. The air seemed filled with them. Their screams were heard from every direction. These birds live mostly on fish, and crumbs which float on the surface of the water. They follow vessels for miles for the refuse thrown overboard.

While I lay here gazing on the mighty deep, I realized what the Poet expressed when he wrote:

"Roll on, thou deep and dark blue ocean, roll;
 Ten thousand fleets sweep over thee in vain;
Man marks the earth with ruin; his control
Stops with the shore; upon the watery plain
 The wrecks are all thy deeds, nor doth remain
A shadow of man's ravage, save thine own
 When for a moment, like a drop of rain,
He sinks into thy depths with bubbling groan,
 Without a grave, unknelled, uncoffined and unknown."

I found large quantities of shell and coral along the shore, which had been washed up from the bed of the ocean. I loaded myself with them and started back for the pony pen. On arriving here I found quite a lively speculation going on in the purchase of those little animals. After the sales were closed, we started back for the boat, once more to wade through the mud. The ponies were put on board the flats, which had reached the shore, it being high tide. Our party took a small boat and sailed down to the steamer, where a fish and champagne dinner was awaiting us. We enjoyed the dinner much, and the table bore witness of the fact when we left it. The boat was still aground, and could not be moved. So a party of six of us took a small boat and set sail for Morehead, leaving the others to enjoy the festivities of the night, which were already running high, owing to the uncorking of too many bottles. We reached our camp shortly after dark. I was much fatigued, and had my fill of pony penning in North Carolina.

The beautiful month of June is with us. The nights and days are mild yet, although the sun has reached its highest altitude. Every tree, plant and shrub, looks fresh and beautiful, which betokens a plentiful harvest to the planter who has cultivated the soil and sown the seed for nature to do its work. This evening I took a stroll along the rifle pits, which extend from Bogue Sound to Calico creek. On my return to camp, much to my surprise, I found my wife, who had just arrived from the North. She had come all the way by water, having been eight days at sea, in a schooner. Four other ladies arrived in camp at the same time, on a visit to their "Liege Lords." We fitted up our tents quite comfortably, and passed a few weeks very pleasantly, leaving the ladies in charge of the camp while we were off on raids, which were of frequent occurrence.

The burning sun of July is now pouring down its most fierce heat. To-night we go on a raid up the Trent river, taking the cars to Newbern. On the morning of the 4th we commenced our march toward Wilmington. We were gone six days, having marched some ninety miles through sand and burning sun, bivouacing along the roads at night. We captured several prisoners, negroes, horses, and a large quantity of stores, having but little fighting with the enemy, returning to camp pretty well used up, most of the men being shoeless.

Our boys had scarcely recovered from their sore feet before we were ordered on a raid up Chowan river, through Hertford county. We took the cars for Newbern, arriving on the banks of the Trent river at midnight, where we cooked three days' rations, after which the troops were put on board of transports, and at daylight sailed down the Neuse river into the Pamlico Sound, passing Fort Hatteras, which is situated on Roanoke Island; thence passing into the Albemarle Sound, where we took in tow some bridges, which were to be used on our expedition. We ascended the Chowan river about sixty miles, and landed our troops near Winton. Our artillery were drawn up the hill by the men and placed in position. Our negro troops soon captured some horses and brought them in, and attached them to the field pieces, which were soon after used on the enemy. At night two thousand cavalry arrived from Portsmouth, by way of Dismal Swamp. They were passed over the Chowan river on the bridges we had brought with us, using our steamboats for butments, they being anchored in the stream, equal distance apart, suitable for the span. In less than two hours we passed over all the cavalry in safety, with their howitzers and stores. This was a feat which has seldom been excelled.

Our infantry visited Winton and Murfreesboro, while our cavalry advanced within ten miles of Weldon, and were driven back by some six thousand rebels, whom they found strongly intrenched at Jackson. Our cavalry made a charge, in which they captured sixty prisoners and two hundred head of horses.

At Winton the infantry encountered some two hundred rebels, and drove them from their breastworks, they leaving tents and equipage behind, which fell into our hands.

Mount Tabor Church stood near by, in a beautiful grove of trees, in which one of our regiments made their quarters during their short stay. Our regiment bivouced in the woods, just beyond the village.

There was a great scarcity of food here, and many of us officers had to resort to foraging on our own account, which was contrary to orders issued, but "necessity knows no law." On one occasion a party of three were privately detailed, on their own application, who guaranteed to furnish all the provisions for our mess the country afforded, on condition that we would protect them against punishment, which was agreed to by the Captain of the company, from which the detail was made, which company was known as the "Forty Thieves."

6

I furnished them transportation, which consisted of a cart and a jackass. The next thing was to pass them through the picket line, which I volunteered to do, and which was very well executed by an understanding with the picket guard, that they were a party after forage for our horses, which came within orders.

The party did not return to camp until late at night, when they were brought in by a guard, who had arrested them as deserters. Their cart, however, was well filled with geese, ducks, chickens, sweet potatoes, &c., which the guard intended to take to the general headquarters. Some of us, who were in the secret of the expedition, parleyed with the guard, while under the cover of night others secreted the contents of the cart in a cornfield near by, unhitched the jack and drove him off into the woods.

Our commanding officer ordered the foraging party to be locked up, after which the guard returned for their booty, but to their disappointment found the contents of the cart had disappeared.

By a little sharp practice, the boys were released during the night, for the purpose of dressing the fowls they had captured and dividing the spoils among those interested, which was done in good faith, and to the satisfaction of all parties.

The next day our commanding officer was invited to dinner. He had played dummy all through the act, and was as "deep in the mud as the boys were in the mire," although they were not cognizant of the fact. I made the remark that I thought he had been rather severe on the boys, whose acts were affording us so much pleasure at present. He at once ordered them to be returned to their company, with the understanding that they were to be tried for violating the articles of war, on their return to camp. The charges against them were never presented by their Captain, and were, of course, forgotten.

While here I was told by one of the natives that Kenneth Raynor had lately made a speech to them, in which he said the Yankees were a set of cowards, and wore not the human form, but had horns protruding from their heads, and that they were incapable of riding a horse or firing a gun. This conversation took place while two thousand of our cavalry were passing (all live Yankees). My Southern friend concluded he had been sold. This is a specimen of the manner in which the Southern people were deceived.

We brought back some three hundred horses, two boat loads of negroes, and seventeen thousand dollars worth of cotton, and about seventy prisoners, returning to Morehead after an absence of eight days, greatly exhausted. I could not really enjoy a hearty meal for nearly a week afterwards.

We found our ladies anxious to see the regiment return, and to know of our safety. We had traveled some eight hundred miles. The country was too impoverished to afford us much of anything to eat, and when we arrived at camp we were nearly starved.

The sultry sun of August makes the atmosphere as "hot as cotton." To-day the news reaches us of the surrender of Fort Wagner, and the destruction of Fort Sumter, but with it comes sad news—the death of our gallant Colonel Shaw, who mounted the parapet and beckoned his colored troops to follow, which they did nobly. He, with many of his officers and soldiers, filled a common grave. That night they were buried beneath the sands of Fort Wagner:

> " And they who for their country die,
>   Shall fill an honored grave ;
> For glory lights the soldier's tomb,
>   And beauty weeps the brave ;
> There is a tear for all who die,
>   A mourner over the humblest grave ;
> But nation swells the funeral cry,
>   And triumph weeps above the brave."

The news of the fall of Fort Sumter will make every free man rejoice. When the first rebel ball smote her rocky sides, the rebound thrilled from shore to shore, and awakened slumbering liberty in every patriot soul. Selfishness and deception disappeared, and patriotism rose from the swelling waves stately as a Goddess.

When shall greatness of soul stand forth, if not in evil times? When the skies are fair and the sea smooth, all ships sail festively, but when the clouds lower, the winds shriek, the waves boil, and soon each craft shows its quality; but here and there a ship rides the storm. Thank God, this great conflict, which for ages has agitated the world, is being fought in our time, that long strife between right and wrong, between freedom and despotism. We are placed in the van-guard. To-day we stand in the thick of the fray and on the enemy's soil.

Shall we let this glorious cause fail? All life has of noble heroic beckons us forward. Death itself bears a golden crown for all who die in freedom's cause, and prizes before which Olympian laurels fade are theirs. This is the year of jubilee, when freemen and slaves march lovingly to meet their fate, and die to save a nation's life.

To-day a year's experience closes, and how checkered it has been. What the next year will bring is hidden in the womb of time; and who would dare draw the vail? A kind Providence has guided my footsteps thus far through the danger, giving me faith and hope of the final triumph of our arms, which cheers me in my darkest and loneliest hours.

Morehead is one of the most healthy locations in the South, situated on a peninsula between Bogue Sound and Calico creek. All through the summer we have a fine breeze from the ocean each day, which renders the air cool and healthful. The cool evenings of September are with us, bringing her purple sunsets and restless winds, making the tall pines which stand like solemn sentinels, sing to us such mournful melodies. For the last two days we have had heavy winds and rain, capsizing many of our tents, leaving the inmates to the mercy of the storm. Last night we had a tremendous gale, so terrific that it awoke me from my slumbers, and compelled me to get up and save my cotton house from capsizing. The storm of last night I shall ever remember, it being the most severe one I have witnessed in camp, during my experience in the army.

Our long expected mail has arrived. We have not received any letters for a month. It brought joy to the camp. In it I found one for myself, which I was glad to receive. It was from my wife, and told me of the news at home and her safe arrival there, and how she found the little ones, and how they clung to her all the day long, for fear she might leave them again to visit Dixie land. Such were the feelings her long absence produced.

Much of a soldier's comfort in camp results from letter communication. Paper and ink are always on hand, or a pencil, which answers the same purpose in the field; this, with a cracker box to write upon, makes a very good secretary. Letters are the links that hold the affections to the home circle, and make absence and trials more easily endured amid the weary marches and rough accommodations of the field. What would we soldiers do without letters? They are the only true heart talkers. The soul measures itself by itself, and tells of truth and love. I re-read my letters carefully when a day is dark and gloomy, and my heart is sick, thinking of all that is unreal and selfish in the world. There, in my camp chest, are many of them bound together; and what a heterogeneous mass of ideas they contain. Some of love, some of hate, some on politics, and some on religion, all so carefully put away that I can find them readily, even in the dark.

To-day a regiment of colored troops arrived at Morehead, from Newbern, called the Second North Carolina Volunteers, all armed and equipped. Their destination was Charleston, South Carolina. I went to the depot where they lay waiting transports, which were soon to convey them to a more active field of operation. The officers were all white, above the rank of sergeant. I conversed with the Chaplain, who was a colored man, and I found him well posted as to the cause of the war and its probable results. He understood the policy of the Government, which many of the Copperheads at the North have not yet learned, and I fear, never will, for "there are none so blind as those who will not see." He thought the Yankees were doing things up right, and that it would be a thorough work, as far as Slavery was concerned, saying that if the institution was saved it would not be worth preserving. I was much pleased with his remarks, believing that he, with many of his race, will live to see his sayings verified. He sagely observed: "What a Yankee leaves undone is not worth finishing."

To-day I visited Beaufort North Carolina, which lay just in sight of our camp, across a beautiful bay, whose waters glisten like sheets of silver on a moon-light night. I took my sail boat, with my darkey pilot, and followed the windings of the channels, which are numerous and difficult to trace, and at low tide very shallow, being almost impossible for the lightest draft boats to pass over the bars.

On my way thither, I saw large white heron on the sand bars, devouring the crabs and small fish which the tide had left behind. There were also wild ducks and mud hens playing around in the water and basking in the sunshine. The bay is filled with shoals, at high tide mostly covered with water, on which immense quantities of rushes grow, which make secure hiding places for those birds to build their nests and hatch their young. During the spring season hunters and fishermen find immense quantities of eggs, which are used for family purposes. The fish caught in these waters are of the finest quality. The mullet is equal to our mackerel at the North.. Clams and oysters are also found in great abundance.

We finally reached Beaufort, after an hour's sail to gain an air line distance of three miles. Such is the channel from Morehead to Beaufort.

The streets of Beaufort are narrow and sandy, with but few shade trees along its walks. Its buildings are mostly old and dilapidated. It has four churches, which present no architectural beauty. It formerly had a large hotel, which extended out into the bay, built on piers; but since our troops landed here the building has been used for a hospital, and contains eight hundred patients. The only thing here that attracted my attention was the snuff dippers. Snuff dipping is practiced by most of the women of the South, also smoking, and they are two of the most filthy habits that can be indulged in by females. The process of dipping is performed by taking a small twig from the black gum tree, battering the end flat, so as to make the fibers into a brush. The snuff is kept in a small tin box, in which the stick is rolled and gathered full of snuff. Then it is swabbed through the mouth. Old snuff dippers may be seen sitting all the day long, with cup in one hand and swab in the other, going through the process, and spitting like a tobacco chewer.

The women look pale and haggard, possessing little vitality, hardly enough to keep themselves looking decent. They are narrow chested and seldom have rosy cheeks, like many of our Northern "lasses." The common classes are very ignorant, and seldom one is found who can read or write.

I returned to my boat and set sail for Fort Macon, which lay just opposite, on the extreme end of an island call Bogue Banks. On my way thither, I passed a small windmill, built on one of the shoals. This antiquated grinding apparatus furnishes the country around with corn meal, from which they make "hoe-cake" and "corn dodgers," which are used instead of bread.

Fort Macon is beautifully located on a rise of ground, mostly artificial in its construction. The access to the fort is by a winding railway and footpath. The fort is built of brick and stone, having an inner and outer terra plain; between them is a moat, which can be filled with water from the sea. The interior has a fine parade, from which you can ascend to the parapet by three stone stairways; both terra plains are mounted with heavy guns; underneath are casemates, all neatly finished off for officers' and soldiers' quarters. Originally, the fort had no terra plain; the guns were mounted in the casemates, the embrasures of which are now used for windows. Here I found all the conveniencies to make the troops comfortable.

From the ramparts you can take a beautiful view of the ocean, and always be fanned by a delightful sea breeze. Here can be seen the gunboats on the blockading squadron plying up and down the coast, from this port to Charleston. Away off to the left are seen Shackleford Banks and Cape Lookout, with its light-house, which stands like a lonely sentinel, with its head of fire, warning the mariner at night from the rocks and shoals he might encounter along this coast.

Away off to the west are seen Burnside's works, from which he shelled this fort in the spring of sixty-two, while our navy made a feigned attack by sea. The marks of the shells are plainly visible, and will remain as a record of the rebellion. I took a stroll up the beach, and passed the breakwater and picket station. About a mile beyond, was Burnside's fortifi-cations, which were loose sand, thrown up at night, behind which his mortars were placed, from which he sent shells so accurately as to drop them into the fort. One of them struck the magazine, which suggested to the inmates the idea of a surrender, before they were all blown up. After a bombardment of eight hours the fort was surrendered to our forces, our troops enter-ing it triumphantly, raising the stars and stripes once more on the spot where they had been taken down and trampled in the dust. The fort is now garrisoned by three companies of the Eighty-First New York Volunteers.

This fort is of much importance, as it commands the entrance to the harbor of Beaufort, and is also a place of confinement for soldiers who have committed military offences. I visited the dungeon where some were confined, where the rays of the sun never enter. It was damp and dismal, and a strange feeling of sadness came over me, as I stood within this dreary cell and heard the murmuring of its inmates. And when its huge doors were swung shut, and the bars grated on my ears, liberty for a moment seemed a mockery.

I left the fort and set sail for camp, being carried along by the tide, which was then setting in, arriving at Morehead just as the last echo of the evening gun died on the distant waters.

This is a beautiful afternoon. The sun is still high in the heavens, with scarcely a cloud to obscure his rays. A gentle sea breeze is blowing from the South, whose cool air is so refreshing. Our camp is as quiet as a New England village on a Sabbath day. After dress parade, the regiment formed a hollow square, and from the center our Chaplain spoke, and the Glee Club sung one of their choice selections, called the "Shining Shore." The music was really charming.

When I returned to my quarters, I found a letter from home, from which I learned my brother had been shot at Ashby Gap, Va., while making a charge. He fell from his horse, most of the squadron passing over him. His comrades, after driving the enemy, returned to bury their dead. They found life in him, and conveyed him back to camp, a distance of fifty miles, where he laid for nearly a week. The surgeon found the ball had entered his skull, near the temple. When able to travel, he was sent home, where the ball was extracted by Dr. Swinburne, some two months afterward, weighing an ounce. He belonged to the California Battalion, attached to the Second Massachusetts Cavalry.

This afternoon I took a ride to Crab Point, on the Newport river. In passing through a pine forest, on my way thither, I saw the negroes gathering pitch from pine trees, for making turpentine. The process is simple. The trees are cut into, about six inches and twelve inches above the base, in a manner which forms a box; then the bark is taken off above, about three feet, in a semi-circular form; from here the pitch exudes and runs into the box below, from which it is taken out, with small wooden dippers, and put into buckets, and then into barrels, which are interspersed through the forest, at the most convenient points for transportation to the factory. Here it is put through a clarifying process, passing through a worm into a large reservoir, in which it is condensed and becomes turpentine. The tar is made from a fat wood, which is put up in kilns, in the form of a cone, and burned, the pitch leaving the wood and running into a gutter formed around the base of the cone or pit; from thence it is dipped up and put in barrels. At present this is a very valuable export for the Northern market, and is a very profitable business for the negro, who has left his master and is working these trees for his own benefit.

As I emerged from the woods, I came on a plantation where I saw some fine fig trees loaded with fruit. I helped myself to them, and found they were the most delicious figs I ever eat. The trees grew from ten to twenty feet high, with very heavy foliage of dark green color, with straggling branches. These trees are great bearers, some yielding as many as ten bushels of this luscious fruit. There are three kinds, red, white and blue. The red is the most delicious, the white is the most hardy, and the blue is the most beautiful. The fig tree bears two crops a year. The first ripens about the first of July. The second one about the first of September, and continues until frost, which comes about the first of November.

Apples, pears, peaches and grapes thrive here, but they are not of such fine quality as we cultivate at the North. The finest varieties could be produced here with little care, but this, like all other Southern States, has the curse of Slavery written on it, and until that is blotted out poverty and destruction must follow. I think many of them begin to realize it already, and the sooner they learn to work and wait on themselves the better it will be for them and their children.

Yankee ingenuity and enterprise is all that is needed to make this "a land flowing with milk and honey," where every one can live under his own vine and fig tree. And if they will become loyal citizens none will molest or make them afraid.

The poor whites and negroes are loyal beyond a doubt, but the slaveholder is not. I have no confidence in their sympathy for Republican institutions. How glad I am to see the noble stand our President has taken against Slavery, with all its horrors, barbarities, and shocking immoralities. Slavery, thank God! is dead in this country, and nothing can resusitate it, and those who now uphold it will perish with it. No friend of human progress will pray for its resurrection. Its destruction was ordained when the Stars and Stripes fell from Fort Sumter. That act was its death knell.

It virtually proclaimed freedom to four millions of human beings, a race who had been held in bondage for more than two centuries.

This morning our surgeon and myself went on a foraging expedition. We took our sail boat and pilot and sailed down Bogue Sound. On our way we met the steamer Guide, having on board conscripts for our army. They were landed at Morehead, and from there took the cars for Newbern. We crossed the Sound for Newport river. On the way up the river we saw large flocks of white and blue heron, which infest these waters; also curlews feeding on the shore. I amused myself by firing at them, and soon found they had no relish for gunpowder. Our route was a very circuitous one, owing to the low tide, which compelled us to go some ten miles to gain an air line distance of three.

We landed at the county almshouse, which is an old dilapidated building, hardly affording shelter fit for beasts It had two inmates, and both of them were insane. I did not learn whether they were insane when they were brought to this miserable hovel, but I am quite certain that their wants and treatment would have a tendency to make them so. Our surgeon observed that he thought the superintendent "non compus mentis." Everything around spoke plainly of poverty; even the corn fields, near by, were incontrovertible witnesses. We left the almshouse with sad impressions.

We strolled off into the country, hoping to find a farmhouse, where we could obtain some refreshment, but all in vain. I purchased some eggs and sweet potatoes at one house; this was all we could procure, after having traveled some four miles.

I made my dinner on raw potatoes, which stayed my hunger for the time. The potatoes were dug by two negro women, whom I found splitting rails for a fence near by. These two slaves were all the help the owner of the plantation had to do his labor. They dug the potatoes with a large plantation hoe, weighing some ten pounds. They had never heard of a potato hook until I described it to them. They "reckoned it must be a right smart thing to dig taters with."

I talked with them in regard to their condition, but they seemed fully satisfied with their prospects, apparently having no desire above their animal wants. I asked the youngest of the two how old she was. She "reckoned about fifteen years." I asked her how much older her mother was than herself. She "reckoned about five years." This is a fair specimen of negro intelligence in many parts of the South. Many mothers do not know the ages of their own children.

We returned to our boats and set sail for the opposite shore. On our way we passed a windmill, grinding corn for hominy and hoecake. One peck of this meal, five pounds of bacon, and one quart of molases, is a week's rations for a man. We passed through, to a wood near by, and took a woodpath which led us to a plantation. After traveling some two miles, through the chapperel and mud, we passed through a field where some negroes were engaged in "saving fodder," as they termed it, which we at the North call topping corn.

I inquired of the darkies the distance to Crab Point, which they told me was "a right smart distance, they reckoned." Near the plantation house was a beautiful grove of fig trees, and a few pomegranate trees, loaded with fruit. I learned from the occupant that he was a deserter from the rebel army. Here he married the woman of his choice, and settled on this plantation, of which she was the owner.

The sun was fast declining in the west, and we put back to our boat, doubling Crab Point just as the flashes of the evening gun were seen from Fort Macon, its echoes rolling along the waters, dying amid the

mellow rays of a Southern sunset, which are beautiful
beyond description.

This afternoon I took a ride back in the country.
As I neared an old farm house, I heard a buzzing
noise, which reminded me of home in my boyhood
days, when I used to teaze my mother to turn the
spinning wheel, and oftentimes destroyed her spindle
of yarn, much to her discomfiture. I unceremoniously
entered the house, and found a girl spinning cotton;
I excused my abruptness, as soldiers generally do, and
took a chair without invitation. She informed me that
she was spinning cotton for a dress, which struck me
as being a very slow process to get one. She told
me she had spun the yarn and wove the cloth of the
dress she then wore, and allowed me the privilege of
examining it. I found it finely spun and finely wove,
and if it had been fitted to her person properly, it
would have looked neat and tidy.

Near by was a cotton field, a most beautiful sight.
The plants grow about four feet high, with numerous
branches. On them were blossoms, green balls and
ripe ones. At this stage the shells burst open, and it
is ready for picking, which commences about the first
of September and continues until the frost kills the
plant. Cotton, after it is picked, is ginned and dried

in the sun, and then pressed into bales. This valuable product can be raised for eight cents per pound.

On my return to camp I was much amused in listening to an account of a panther hunt in the wilds of Northern New York. The hero of this story is a soldier in our regiment. He said:

"Some years ago, in the month of January, early in the morning, I went out to find my• sheep. On finding my flock I missed some of them, and on looking around discovered traces which convinced me some animal had visited my flock at night and carried off some of them for their prey. I returned home for my gun, and told my wife where I was going; I also told her to request two of my neighbors to follow up my trail. I traveled all day, and when night came, bivouaced, building a fire to guard me from any attack from the foe I was in search of. The long and weary night passed in earnest thoughts and longing desires for the first glimpses of daylight. Morning dawned at last, and after a lunch. from my hunting bag, I resumed my journey and traveled until late in the afternoon, when I heard a shrill echo resounding through the forest, telling me my dogs had found their prey. With cautious steps and trembling limbs I

advanced in the direction of the sound, and soon came
in sight of the dogs, who were at the base of a large
tree, anxiously waiting for their master.   As I neared
the tree I gazed up and saw on one of the limbs a
monstrous panther, lying in an attitude of readiness
to spring at any moment.   Now came the trying time
for me to quiet my nerves, as every muscle seemed
unstrung.   The others had arrived in sight which
gave me more confidence and coolness, qualities so
essential at such a moment.   I beckoned to them to
come up, and be ready to fire.   At that moment I
sent a ball whizzing through the head of the animal,
striking him in the mouth, which left him minus one
tooth, and bleeding freely.

"The animal lay looking at me with eyes of fire,
showing clearly that his nature had been wrought up
to a fierce anger.   The two others fired while I loaded
my gun, the balls striking him near the heart, at which
they aimed, seemingly without effect.   The ninth shot
brought him reeling to the ground, writhing in agony.
One of the dogs attacked him, and with one stroke of
his claw the panther tore the dog to pieces, killing him
instantly, and at the same moment the panther expired.

"We cut a rail and tie dour prize to it, carrying him
on our shoulders over a mile, to a farm house where

we weighed him and found we had one hundred and eighty-seven pounds of panther flesh, including skin and bone. From here we conveyed him to Utica in a wagon, and from thence to Albany, by railroad, where he was purchased by a taxidermist, who skinned and stuffed him in the best manner, so true to nature that to-day he appears to be alive, standing on all fours, as he once did when he roamed over his native forest."

I have reason to believe that there is truth in this story, as a friend of mine was presented with some of the panther steak, and shared it with me at the time. The recollection of the deliciousness of the meat gave additional zest to the tale.

Another story was related by a member of another regiment. He said:

"About fifty of us had been engaged for several days in performing secret service, and were on our return. We had to pass very near the rebel lines, and to avoid being taken, and also to save a circuit of miles, we resolved to encamp in a secluded place we knew of, through the day, and under the shadow of night pass unseen on the direct course to our camp,

The day was beautiful, and the spot we had chosen for our resting place was one of those grassy nooks, shut out apparently from the rest of the world by lines

of hills, impenetrable underbrush, and a gigantic forest;
a small but clear and deep stream ran by it. We lay
down our arms, relieved ourselves of our knapsacks,
and spreading our provender upon the grass, dined
with a hearty appetite, refreshing ourselves from the
limpid waters of the stream, and then each one amused
himself as best he could.

"After resting awhile, some one of the party went
in to bathe, and one by one, as the pleasure seemed to
increase, followed, until the whole party were in the
stream. This lasted for about half an hour, and most
of us had returned to the shore, and were dressing, when
a new feature was given to the scene by one of the
party saying he was going to wash his shirt. Now
most of us had worn these garments for some time
without washing, and there could be no doubt of their
needing it very much. We all thought the idea a good
one, and all hands immediately began to disrobe, and
soon we were as busy as washerwomen, rubbing away
like fulling mills. As the pieces were finished they
were hung on the limbs of trees, in the sun, or spread
out on the grass.

"Many were still engaged at their washing; some
were stretched on the ground in deep sleep, some were
wrestling, others jumping, and some collected in groups,

telling stories, nearly all of us innocent of wearing apparel as Adam was previous to forming acquaintance with Eve, and about as happy as fellows could be, with but one shirt, and that drying in the sun, when we were startled by a volley of musketry, the balls of which, very fortunately, only made a few slight flesh wounds.

"The sound of musketry, although it surprised us at first, we were too much accustomed to hearing, to remain long under a panic; so the next moment found each man of us in possession of his musket, and himself covered by a tree. We had not long to wait, before a large body of rebels broke through the underbrush, which had concealed them, and charged with fixed bayonets upon us. But their progress was suddenly checked by our fire, which laid a number of them dead. We had not time to reload, when the enemy charged down upon us, and we were compelled reluctantly to give way. We ran some distance, reloading, and stood our ground.

"Up to this time we had not thought of our nude condition, until one of our officers cried: 'Boys, will you lose your shirts?' Then, casting our eyes around, we gave a shout: 'Now for our shirts!' and rushed forward like so many naked devils.

"As soon as the enemy came to our view, we poured in a well directed fire, and immediately charged with the bayonet. So suddenly had this movement been made, that, having supposed we were still running away, they in turn were completely surprised, and then came their turn to run. After them we shouted still, with our new watchword, "Shirts!" The officers of the enemy, having at length succeeded in securing the attention of their men, wheeled them, and gave us a return fire, when we again took to our heels, and the rebels, taking up our cry of "Shirts!" came pell-mell after us. Again we turned and charged the enemy running, and they in turn charging upon us, each party shouting 'Shirts!'

At length, becoming somewhat exasperated with the game, and constantly reminded of our shirts, by the enemy screaming it in our ears, and recollecting, too, that we would not cut a very pretty figure returning to quarters *sans culottes*, we made a most desperate charge, and finally succeeded in gaining the day, driving the enemy from the field. Several of our party were wounded, but none killed, and putting on our garments, we took the circuitous route which we had avoided in the morning, and reached camp about midnight, where we caused no little merriment when we related our adventure, in which our shirts so narrowly escaped capture."

In this way many a long evening is passed in camp. Most soldiers have some tale to tell, of hunting, fishing, or encounters they have met with on picket, or the battle field, and they are most generally the hero of their own story.

Last evening the wind blew a perfect gale; so hard that it kept me awake nearly all night. The mighty waves were rolling in the distance, against the breakwaters on the shore of Bogue Banks. The roar told me of a terrible storm at sea. During the night a vessel had been driven ashore on Bogue Banks, and became imbedded in the sand. The waves were dashing over her, making her a total wreck. The crew had just abandoned her, and floated to shore on spars.

Their cargo consisted principally of sugar and rum, which, after the storm had abated, was taken off, by cutting out the sides of the vessel, and carried away on lighters. I visited the crew on the beach; they told me they were from Cuba, bound for New York, and had lost their course in the storm during the night. They were a miserable set of men, being half Spaniard and half negro, looking more like a band of pirates than English tars, under which flag they sailed. A few days afterward a Captain of one of our gunboats told me he had chased this craft for two days, off the coast of Wilmington, North Carolina, and that when he crowded them they threw cannon overboard. He was satisfied they were blockade runners, although their papers showed to the contrary.

Our regimental inspection came off to-day. The men and equipments were in fine order. The regiment passed in review, and were highly complimented for their military appearance.

After inspection, I found a notice at my quarters, which required me to attend a court martial at Newbern, where I was required to appear as a witness. the following day. I took the cars in the evening for that place, which is situated thirty-five miles from the coast. I spent the night with one of the surgeons of the Ninety-Second New York Volunteers, who was an old friend. The next morning I visited Fort Stephenson, on the banks of the Neuse river. It has three guns, and is garrisoned by one company of the Third Massachusetts Artillery.

Just across the Neuse is Fort Anderson, which was attacked by the rebels, under General Pettigrew, last spring. It was then garrisoned by the Ninety-Second New York Volunteers, who nobly defended it, without firing a shot; their guns not being mounted, they awaited the charge of the enemy, who kept up a constant fire of grape, canister and shell, for some time, destroying the quarters within the fort. In the meantime Colonel Anderson, who commanded the fort, signaled to Newbern for assistance. A gunboat soon came to his relief, which drove the enemy back, and Fort Anderson was saved.

Newbern is situated at the intersection of the Neuse and Trent rivers, and compares well with most of the Southern cities in point of size. It has a number of fine residences surrounded with beautiful gardens, in which are generally found grapes, figs, pears and pomegranates; also abundance of flowering shrubs, such as honeysuckle, myrtle, magnolia, and the Rose of Sharon. There are no curiosities of nature or art here, except a kind of rock taken from the bed of the Trent river, whose formation is composed of shells, which is used for fence and building purposes, and resembles vermulated ashler.

They have the same blue sky and twinkling stars above them that we have at the North, but not those noble mountains, with their deep gorges and silvery cascades we have on the Hudson, and through some parts of New England. The country, as far as the eye can reach, is one vast pine forest. This is the geographical character of the South, along the seaboard, extending some fifty miles back.

The battle field of Newbern lays about four miles east of the city, between the Goldsboro Railroad and the Neuse river. General Burnside drove the rebels from that field to Newbern, and from there they retreated to Kinston, setting fire to the bridge which crossed the Trent river, after they had passed over it; but our troops soon came up and extinguished the flames. They also set fire to the city, which was extinguished before much damage was done.

Newbern is at present strongly fortified, having fortifications running from the Neuse to the Trent river; before those works were built, it required about fifteen thousand troops to hold this place, but I am of opinion that the Government would have been better off to have burned these places, when taken, than to fortify and hold them, as they have done, even if they were obliged to rebuild them. It is a great expense to hold an inland city, and has a tendency to make a department inactive, on account of accommodations it affords the officers.

I returned to Morehead, in company with the Third Massachusetts Artillery, who were to relieve a detachment of the Eighty-First Regiment New York Volunteers, at Fort Macon.

A bright and beautiful October morning, with its hazy sunshine and yellow leaves, tells me a change in the year is already at hand. The heavy dew and cool nights admonish us that the greatcoat and rubber blanket will soon be needed, to prevent the chills and fever, which is so common at this time of year in the South.

The brig Release has just arrived in harbor, in which Dr. Kane was brought home on his last journey to the Arctic regions. She is now a gunboat, and is connected with the blockading squadron. I visited her, and while on board, the mate told me she had been remodeled since her cruise to the North Pole. I felt pleased to tread her deck, because she had released one of our country's adventurers from those frozen regions of the North, where he had been bound up in the ice, with his vessel, the Advance, for many months, only to meet his death and find a grave in a more genial clime, beside his kindred. He died in early manhood; but his memory will live eternal as those hills of ice, in which he spent so many cheerless months, and sunless days, with the natives of those regions and his Arctic voyagers.

Our Chaplain and myself took a sail to Shackleford Banks, and visited the fishermen, whom we found hard at work, cleaning fish and putting them in barrels; in one haul they caught one hundred and thirty barrels. High noon had arrived, and we began to feel hungry, so we started off in the wood, and found a grove of cedars, underneath which we spread our cloth on the sand, and partook of a hearty repast from our haversack. After satisfying our hunger, we went in search of grapes and chinkpins, a kind of nut which grows here; we had to make our way through a thick chaparral, on all fours, for nearly half a mile, with the pleasant idea of coming in contact with snakes and lizards, without speaking of the mutilation to our clothing. I at last found a beautiful vine; it clung to a large oak, and in the top hung large clusters of fine grapes, ripening in the sun.

I laid off my haversack and canteen, and got into the tree with much difficulty, the vines being woven together. I accomplished my object, and soon satisfied my appetite with grapes, which I found to be very delicious; I then dropped myself down again with less trouble than I had in getting up, yet not without some scars.

Here, in these woods, grows a fine quality of muscadine grapes, equally as sweet and large as those cultivated at the North, but not in such large clusters. We whiled away an hour in the woods, and after some trouble got out, taking the sun for our guide.

The fishermen live principally in huts, in which I saw poverty and ignorance, such as I could not believe existed, if I had not witnessed it; for it had almost run into insanity. They were really heathens; and this in "Free America," as it is called. I told our Chaplain if any place on God's footstool needed missionaries, this was the spot. I asked one of the women if she did not get lonesome, living on this island; she "reckoned right smart." The whole family did not appear to have any knowledge above their animal wants.

We took our boat and floated back with the tide to camp, just as the sun sank beneath the distant waters; when we received orders to be ready, at a moment's notice, to proceed to Fortress Monroe, on the arrival of transports from that place.

The One Hundred and Fifty-Eighth New York Volunteers have just arrived from Newbern, to relieve us; they are a rough looking regiment, having some three hundred sick, and the remainder hardly fit for duty. Our camp is all excitement now—especially among the officers' wives. Packing up is the order of the day. Since we have received orders to be ready, it has rained, accompanied with much thunder and lightning.

The waves of the ocean are keeping up a continual murmur, which makes melancholy music, and the pattering rain falling on my tent, makes one feel gloomy and lonesome. How true it is that the weather and seasons affect our minds; our natures are so much in sympathy with them.

Our last act at Morehead was to release from bondage a negro family. About a mile from our camp were held a colored man's wife and four children, as slaves—the master forbidding the husband visiting them. The husband complained to our Colonel of their treatment, and assured him they were held against their wishes.

The master was summoned to appear the next day at our headquarters, at a certain hour, which he failed to do, but the negro was on hand, and insisted upon having his wife and children.

Our Adjutant volunteered to rescue the negro family from bondage. I furnished him with transportation and off they started through a heavy rain storm, as there was no time to lose, for we were momentarily expecting to leave North Carolina. Half an hour's ride brought him to the plantation; they found the negroes overjoyed at the thought of being released from that despotism which had enchained them during their lives. The old matron and daughters "showed fight." The officer told them to keep quiet, as he was there in the discharge of his duty, and did not wish to be charged with shooting a woman, but the negroes should have their freedom at any sacrifice. The husband picked out his wife and children; they were put in the wagon, with their luggage, and left the plantation amid the curses and groans of the mistress.

At midnight we received orders to strike our tents at daylight, and get aboard transports at sunrise. Long before day the boys commenced tearing down and burning up, and at daylight our camp presented a scene of desolation.

We are now leaving the dock, with flying colors, for the briny deep; the boys are jolly, and many of them well filled with whisky, which is a great curse to most of the men and officers. At sundown the land lay in the distance, hardly visible to the naked eye. The moon is high in the heavens, yet in her crescent form, making the ocean look like billows of silver; a fine, steady breeze is blowing from the south, as if to urge us on to our destined port, which is Old Point Comfort.

Many on board are sick, and not able to keep their dinner, for which they have just paid. I feel quite uneasy myself, but am determined not to yield to the sickening influences of the vessel. It is midnight, and the last pale ray of the moon has disappeared; darkness and silence surrounds us; our vessel plows steadily through the waves, leaving a track of fire behind her.

The gray morning is at last breaking, and I am the first on deck, to greet the "God of day," as he comes peeping up from the eastern waters, throwing his rays in every direction.

The sand banks which skirt the shores of North Carolina are again in view, but lay away so far that they appear like a dark cloud on the horizon; we soon came in full view of the sandy beach; away off to the west stands the lighthouse off Cape Henry; we now enter the great harbor, and see Virginia's shores on either side.

Directly in front of us stands Fort Wool, known as the Rip Raps. We passed under its guns, and came to anchor. Our Colonel reported to General Foster, who commanded the Department of Virginia and North Carolina, who ordered our brigade to encamp at Newport News, which is situated on the James river, about six miles above the Fortress.

Newport News is situated on a high bluff, and just opposite, in the river, lay the Cumberland and Congress, in which an hundred seamen found a watery grave; they stood by their guns so long that many found it impossible to gain the upper deck, and went down with their gallant ship, standing by the flag of their country. The river is about four miles wide, with a channel deep enough for the largest vessels to sail in.

Opposite is seen the waters of the Elizabeth and Nansemond rivers; on the former lays Portsmouth and Norfolk, and on which also Gosport Navy Yard is situated, which was burned in the early part of the rebellion, to prevent the rebels from taking it. At the mouth of these rivers lay the gunboats Roanoke, Cambridge, and Minnesota. The former is a three-turreted monitor. These vessels form the blockading squadron on the James river.

One of the greatest luxuries we have here at Newport News is plenty of good water; which I have not tasted before in seven long months. One of the greatest hardships which our army suffers is to be deprived of water, and it is probably the main cause of fever.

The autumn leaves are falling, and the hazy sunshine of November gives timely warning of approaching winter. I took a walk along the James river, above our camp; on my way I passed a graveyard, where lay some of the defenders of our country, some of those who died in the early part of the Peninsula campaign. As I gazed on those little mounds, sad feelings came over me; they were the graves of the illustrious dead, our country's heroes, who had fallen by the wayside, while hope and faith glimmered in the future.

Only eighteen months ago one hundred and thirty thousand men had passed this point, on their way to Richmond, full of hope, and love of country, to inspire them on their toilsome march. But a sad record is told along the road. Not less than thirty thousand found their graves on this peninsula. Here they rest in peace, free from toil and care, nor do the ravages of war disturb them, for they have fought their last battle.

The sun was fast disappearing behind the western forests, as I turned reluctlantly from a spot so sacred, and full of historic reminiscences; aside from these associations, the scenery in view was magnificent beyond description, bathed as it then was in the golden sunset, which made it doubly beautiful. I could not resist the temptation to linger there until the twilight shades deepened into night.

This morning our Major, Chaplain, and myself, mounted our horses and rode over to Hampton, a distance of seven miles from our camp; the day was warm and beautiful, the forest leaves were dyed with many different colors, and showed plainly that a frost had visited them; but on our way, as we rode across the fields, we saw many wild flowers still in full bloom, which reminded us of the month of June.

We arrived at Hampton, after an hour's ride. The first building we saw was the remains of an old Episcopal church, which is said to have been built over two hundred years ago; its porch had fallen, but the gables and side walls yet stand, a monument of rebel barbarity. The building was built in Roman style, and in form of a Latin cross; the grounds in which it stands are enclosed with a brick wall, well studded with weeping willows, and like most ancient church-

yards, had been used for burial purposes by those pro-
fessing the faith.

This was once a delightful spot, but now the
ravages of war has made it desolate; its monuments
thrown down, and the slabs which cover the last resting place of the honored dead are broken, and many
of the inscriptions defaced. I sat down by a tomb
whose inscription bore the date of 1701, a date which
carried my mind back one hundred and sixty-two
years. From this spot I took a sketch of the old
church, after which we left our horses in charge of a
negro boy, and took a walk about the village. Most
of the buildings had been burned by the American
vandals, and the burnt spots were being supplanted
by negro shanties, which were built here in great
numbers. We stepped into one of them, and found
an oyster vender; we partook freely of the bivalves.
They were the finest I ever ate. After we had worried
the darkey some twenty minutes in opening them, we
paid him his bill, which was only fifty cents. Oysters
are found in great abundance in the bay, near by,
and are often sold at the rate of fifty cents per gallon,
solid meats.

We returned to camp just in time to miss our
dinner, which was quite a disappointment to us, after

order. It also contains two hotels, the National and Atlantic. In a sitting room of one of these hotels, I saw a bill posted, notifying the guests that no political discussions would be allowed, either in the house or on the stoop. While there I saw many seedy old gentlemen hanging around, who appeared to belong to the F F V's, and it seemed to me they had seen better days. Their threadbare coats and old fashioned hats bespoke a loss that none understood as well as themselves; their hats appeared to be at least ten years behind the age, and those who wore them, at least fifty; they were men not fit for the rebel service, and were left to take care of the women and children, many of whom are now widows and orphans.

Norfolk and Richmond were the principal slave markets. Here, before the rebellion, could be seen the whipping post and slave pens; also the father and mother, with their children, brought to market and sold from their masters, like sheep, to be separated forever; and this in a land where we have boasted so many years: That all men were born free and equal, and endowed with certain inalienable rights; among them life, liberty, and the pursuit of happiness. Thank God! that day is past. Many of those slaves are now Union soldiers, and are helping to fight the battles of our country. I returned to camp much pleased with my visit to Norfolk.

This evening (Nov. 17th) our regiment received marching orders, to be ready to embark on board of transports, bound for Portsmouth. We had our stores and equipage on board in due time, and on arriving there, received orders to go to Northwest Landing.

I transferred my stores on board of a barge, and was towed up the Elizabeth river, entering the Albemarle and Chesapeake Canal, near Great Bridge, while the regiment took the road on foot. In going up we went through a desolate country, and passed the mouth of the Dismal Swamp Canal, which unites the waters of the Elizabeth with the Pasquotank river, and empties into Albemarle Sound, making water communication with Elizabeth City, North Carolina.

We passed the mouth of the canal just at sundown. As the twilight disappeared, the moon came peeping up from behind the thick forests of Dismal Swamp, and afforded us a beautiful light for our journey. Through this dreary region all was quiet, not a murmur, even from the toads, was heard. It was quite cool, and ere midnight I was compelled to get up and rub my limbs to keep warm. Long looked for daylight appeared at last, and we went ashore and built a fire, by which we warmed ourselves. Our regiment had bivouaced near by us, in the woods, and were ready to continue their march to Northwest Landing, a distance of fifteen miles across the country, which was infested by guerillas. Eleven wagons were loaded with camp equipage, and followed the regiment; I left a guard of twenty men in charge of the balance of the stores. We reached Northwest Landing at dark. When within a mile of the place two soldiers, who were in advance of the guard, were suddenly attacked by some guerillas; one was shot, the other taken prisoner. The regiment bivouaced for the night in a pine grove, at a place called Plug's Hills. Here we built winter quarters.

Thanksgiving has arrived, and we have kept it much to our credit, in these backwoods of Virginia. In the morning the regiment was formed in a hollow square. Our Adjutant read a letter from Governor Seymour; also his proclamation. The Chaplain offered up a prayer, the Glee Club sang, and the drum corps played Hail Columbia, after which the Chaplain made a few appropriate remarks on the war and its prospects. The exercises closed with Yankee Doodle.

At two o'clock we sat down in a beautiful pine grove, having a rustic table built, well loaded with the good things of this life, such as turkeys, geese, ducks, chickens, quail, sweet potatoes, tomatoes, cabbage, and other vegetables, with plenty of ale, and pumpkin pie. The day was cool and pleasant, and will long be remembered by us all, as the Thanksgiving dinner in the backwoods of Virginia, near Dismal Swamp.

Bleak November is drawing to a close; to-day is Sunday, and I am ordered to Norfolk for supplies. Myself, teams, and a cavalry escort, started through the storm, riding a distance of twenty-five miles, arriving in Norfolk after dark. It was the hardest half day's journey I have experienced in the army, and I was too tired to sleep soundly, even on a feather bed, which would have been a luxury under other circumstances.

December comes in mild and beautiful, much like our delightful Indian summers at the North, although the long nights are cold and cheerless in our old and much worn canvas houses.

Our camp is situated in a pine grove, which was once a cornfield, the hills of which are plainly visible. On this spot some Tories were hung during the Revolution, they having given the enemy information as to the movements of our army, at that time.

Some three miles from here is an old brick church, which was erected one hundred and fifty years ago. The roof has fallen in, and its walls are covered with moss, which show solidity, after having stood the storms of so many years.

In this region of country there is plenty of game, such as bears, wild cat, quail, squirrels, &c. I was awakened by the cry of a wild cat, last night; he made the forest ring with his screams, making night hideous. This is a dense wilderness, our camp lying on the borders of Dismal Swamp, whose waters flow into the Northwest river, and is called juniper, which shrub is abundant in this swamp, making the water of a red color, and it is considered a healthy drink.

This great swamp covers an area of some three hundred square miles, Lake Drummond being in the center of it, from which Dismal Swamp Canal is fed. The cypress and cedar grow very large here. Juniper is found in abundance, and woodbine grows wild and rank, clinging to every shrub and tree within its reach.

This was formerly a great rendezvous for the runaway negroes. Some would remain secreted here for months, living on game and roots. In the season when corn is fit for use, they would travel miles to obtain it, and return again to their hiding places before daybreak.   The bloodhounds were often used for hunting out these poor creatures, and when found many were shot before they would be captured.   I was told this by one who had experienced it.   In the same conversation he said his master told him he could not take care of himself, if given his liberty.   He told him he was willing to try the experiment, as he and his family had from their labor supported both themselves and their master and his family; he also remarked: "Now, I say, let the negro have his freedom, and if he wont work let him 'root hog or die,' dese ar my sentiments."

A story is told of a young man who lost his mind, upon the death of a girl he loved, and who suddenly disappearing from his friends, was never afterwards heard of.   As he had frequently said, in his ravings, that the girl was not dead, but gone to the Dismal Swamp, it is supposed he had wandered into that dreary wilderness, and had died from hunger, or got lost in some of its dreadful morasses.

The celebrated poet, Tom Moore, while on a visit to this country, hearing the above related, composed the following verses, which give a truthful description of this dismal region:

Away to the Dismal Swamp he speeds—
 His path was rugged and sore,
Through tangled juniper, beds of reeds,
Through many a fen, where the serpent feeds,
 And man never trod before.

And when on the earth he sunk to sleep,
 If slumber his eyelids knew,
He lay, where the deadly vine doth weep
Its venomous tear and nightly steep
 The flesh with blistering dew:

And near him the she-wolf stirr'd the brake,
 And the copper-snake breathed in his ear,
'Till he starting cried, from his dream awake,
"Oh! when shall I see the dusky Lake,
 And the white canoe of my dear?"

He saw the Lake, and a meteor bright
 Quick over its surface play'd—
"Welcome," he said, "my dear one's light,"
And the dim shore echoed, for many a night,
 The name of the death-cold maid.

'Till he hollow'd a boat of the birchen bark,
 Which carried him off from shore;
Far, for he follow'd the meteor spark,
The wind was high and the clouds were dark,
 And the boat returned no more.

But oft, from the Indian hunter's camp,
 This lover and maid so true
Are seen at the hour of midnight damp,
To cross the Lake by a fire-fly lamp,
 And paddle their white canoe.

Our flag presentation took place to-day. The regiment was formed in a hollow square, and our Colonel stated briefly the object of the parade. The drum corps played the Star Spangled Banner, when the flag was brought forward and Captain Ballard made the following presentation remarks:

"*Colonel, Officers and Soldiers of the 81st Regiment:*

"The morning I left home for the regiment, I was handed one hundred dollars by Mr. Ingersoll, of Lee, Oneida county, to purchase a flag for our regiment. It was an unexpected event, to me, and in my embarrassment and thankfulness I am afraid I did not make a suitable acknowledgment for the gift.

"It may be proper here for me to say a few words in regard to Mr. and Mrs. Ingersoll, for I apprehend they are in company in this, as they are in every other good work, although but one of their names appears in the letter of presentation.

"The great Sahara of human selfishness and avarice is all dotted with green and fertile spots, where the weary traveler finds encouragement, refreshment and repose, and the remembrance remains in his heart. The home of the ones who make this gift is one of the oases in life's desert, among the many who are half disloyal, among the many who make noisy, but empty professions of their faith in our final triumph. They are those who show their faith by their works; they are emphatically, and devotedly, the friend of the soldier and the soldier's family. In their homes are shown what age, youth and woman can do, when inspired by patriotism and a love of right, to help preserve our National life. From the first outbreak of the rebellion their hands and purses have been the servants of their prayers. The dearest object of their affections has not been counted too dear for an offering to their country. It is not an exaggeration, when I affirm that in this struggle had every Northern man, and every Northern woman, worked with a zeal and an energy like theirs, before this time war's bloody tide would have been stayed, and thousands who have perished, and will yet perish on the battle field, might have been spared, to bring comfort and gladness to their homes.

"It has been said that 'A thing of beauty is a joy forever.' The American flag is a thing of beauty; beautiful in its chaste simplicity; beautiful because it is the emblem of Liberty, Union, Justice, and Equality; and there is an additional beauty imparted to it when presented as now, in this our country's hour of peril and trial, by those who possess loyal hearts.

"We are in arms to-day to fight, if necessary, that the flag may retain its proud pre-eminence among the nations of the earth, and that it may be a joy forever, to all people, even to those who shall till the fertile fields of the South. By every effort in its power, in the future as in the past, may the Eighty-First see to it—in regard to our country and its free institutions, in regard to our gallant dead, in regard to the loyal living at home, in the field and on the sea, in regard to future generations, and the estimable lady who makes us this gift, may the Eighty-First New York see to it that no dishonor stains its folds."

To which our Colonel made the following reply:

" *Captain Ballard:*

"In behalf of the regiment which I have the honor to command, allow me to say that I was not a little surprised and delighted on hearing from you that we had in our very camp, surrounded as we are by the enemies of our country, a new and beautiful 'Star Spangled Banner;' coming as it does at this opportune moment, being destitute of a suitable banner around which to rally in the hour of battle, and at a distance from the headquarters of the Department to which we are attached, and in sight of those who would trample it under their feet, should the opportunity offer, which may God forbid. By the strong arm of the Eighty-First New York, it is more than welcome.

"That flag presented to us by a representative of the fair sex, will be doubly dear to us; it being an emblem of the Union of States not only, but of 'hearts and hands.' Every time we gaze on its azure field, may we call to mind our brothers, wives, sweethearts and sisters that we have left behind, and remember that we, in defending that ensign, are protecting from invasion the firesides of our loved ones at home.

In accepting this National emblem from Mrs. E. C. Ingersoll, in behalf of my command, I can but feebly express to her, through you, our heartfelt thanks and gratitude for this donation at this time; no one thing could be received by us of more importance; and I trust that each and every member of this regiment will consecrate himself anew to the work in which we are engaged; and may this beautiful flag never be polluted by the touch of traitor hands.

"And now, fellow soldiers, one and all, it remains for you to say whether this flag, respected and honored by all the nations of the earth, far and near, shall be saved from disgrace at home. Your silence tells me in language not to be mistaken that each of you, if needs be, will lay down his life to defend it to the last from enemies abroad and traitors at home.

"Captain, I thank you, we all thank you, and that Heaven's choicest blessing may descend on the donor is the fervent prayer of him who has the honor to lead this 'noble band of our country's defenders.'"

The flag was then placed in the hands of Sergeant Michels, of Company E.

On motion of our Surgeon, three cheers were given for the flag, after which the Chaplain asked a blessing on the donor and the regiment, in future. The companies were ordered to their respective street, and stood at "parade rest" while the drum corps played the sunset retreat, to the tune of Sweet Afton. The scene was beautiful, the music most charming, and when its last echo had died far away amid the lofty cedars and twining woodbine of Dismal Swamp, we returned to our quarters and partook of a hearty supper which our French cook had prepared for us.

Our regiment becoming short of rations, obliged us to resort to foraging. A detail was made and put under the command of an officer, who went out some three miles from our camp and captured a number of hogs and beef cattle. They were owned by a disloyal citizen, named Wilson, who protested against having them slaughtered, as they were all he had for his winter's use, and he was much afraid he would starve if they were taken. We told him necessity knew no law, and without further parleying, the hogs were shot. The boys yoking the cattle to his cart and wagon brought them to camp, where they were skinned, dressed and distributed to the different companies. In the meantime Wilson went to Norfolk and took the oath of allegiance. A few days after he came to our camp and asked pay for his property. I told him that we did not pay cash, but would give him a receipt for the number of pounds of pork and beef received, in the name of the United States Government, which he seemed willing to take. Across the face of the receipt I wrote, with red ink, "disloyal citizen" which he at the time did not notice. After he returned home he examined it more closely, and found he had been classed as a rebel, which did not seem to suit him. The next morning he came to my quarters and asked me to change the receipt, as he had taken the oath of allegiance. I told him I could not do that, for at the time his property was taken he recognized the Confederate Government as paramount to the one at Washington, which I represented. He left with a sad countenance, seeming to think his receipt would be of little use—a wiser, if not a better man.

The clouds look gray to-day, and the air is chilly, indicating the approach of a cold storm. Our men have commenced rebuilding the bridge across Northwest river, which will take some days to complete.

This afternoon, while writing, I heard martial music in the distance, which soon aroused the whole camp. An officer came galloping in, and announced to us the arrival of the 5th United States colored troops, on their way to North Carolina. The music sounded beautiful, which was to the tune of "We are marching along." One company of black zouaves accompanied them as far as our camp. This company was drumming up recruits for the 10th Virginia regiment, which was then being organized at Norfolk. Their dress is very attractive, which induces many to join their ranks.

The negroes are flocking around the old flag by hundreds; soon we shall have an army of them, sufficient to cope with the thinned ranks of the rebels. They make good soldiers, can endure hardships and privations, and love Liberty and their homes.

"The naked negro panting on the line,
    Boasts of his golden sands, and palmy wine;
    Such is the patriot's boast where e'er we roam;
    His first, best country, ever is his own."

This afternoon the Surgeon, Chaplain and myself, took a ride on horseback, about two miles beyond our picket and videt posts, to a place called Hickory Ground; on our return we found a grove of persimmon trees, which were loaded with fruit. I rode under one of the trees, stood on my saddle, and ate my fill.

They are of a most delicious flavor when ripe; but before they are matured, the most bitter fruit I ever tasted; the trees resemble the hickory, and the fruit that of small rotten apples, the flavor; that of a date. The natives here use the fruit for beer; and it is said to be good for fevers.

On our return we took a by-road, which brought us out of the woods in sight of a small house. We drove up to the door and found it was occupied by two ladies, who had just commenced housekeeping; they invited us to call again, when they got settled.

We drove down the road bout half a mile, and returned on a full gallop, soon reaching the woods, just beyond the house. A few moments after one of our officers was fired on from the rear of the house. No doubt the Bushwhacker was in the house at the time we were conversing with the ladies.

That night a scouting party of fifty men went out about eight miles, as far as Indian Creek, and at daylight arrested a number, and brought them into camp for examination, but could find no clue to the enemy.

To-night is cold and cheerless; the moon shines brightly, and nought is heard except the sentinel's tread as he walks his lonely beat. In these silent hours of the night the heart wanders back to home and loved ones there, but soon returns, unsatisfied with imaginative enjoyment, and then it dreams of its early boyhood and the fond associations of those dreamy days of youth when wandering along the banks of the Mohawk in my native valley; all those fond recollections come pressing upon my mind. What would I not give were it possible to recall back one hour—one single hour—over whose memory many tears have been shed. How I would love to view again those pleasant scenes where I was delighted, before hope was seen glimmering through a dark and misty future.

To-night the old school house presents itself to my mind, with its windbreaks of pines which surround it, and the fleshy and jolly old schoolmaster, who used his whip so freely over our backs, to make us respect his position. Near by was a little cottage hemmed in by trees, and underneath the shades of one was an old well with its "Old Oaken Bucket," from which I have drank many a draft of cool water on a hot summer's day; here once lived a happy heart, now passed away.

I see the old mill, with its brook still serenely flowing—the old miller long since gone to rest; there is my native city in the distance, lying quietly among the hills that skirt the Mohawk, with its tall spires silently tracing life's changeful story, and pointing to those who have fled and gone to rest; further on, in the distance, I see the river moving in silent majesty, on its way to the sea; on the hillside is the old family graveyard, where lies the remains of one who was dear, and around which spot my heart still clings. It is my mother's grave. Near by my little sister rests; it is long since she died; yet the scenes are fresh before me; how plainly I see her still, and methinks I am wandering with her on the play ground, but which is no longer pleasant, for the happy heart that enjoyed it so fully has passed forever from my sight. The trees have grown old; the flowers have faded and withered, and I shall see their bright smiles no more.

The remembrance of by-gone days, almost destroys my happiness; vainly have I hoped to still the murmurings of my heart, forgetting in the stern realities of the present, those fond days of the past; still hope is with me, and when every tie that binds me to earth is broken, when life appears a dreary waste, and every stream that feeds the heart is dried up, still this magic fountain continues to play, whose murmurs are music to my weary soul.

I hear stray shots on our picket line. The long roll is sounded, which brings our regiment into line, and four companies are dispatched to different points. The following morning brought us the news that a large rebel force had crossed at South Mills, on the Pasquatank river, and were advancing on General Wilde, whose colored brigade were raiding through that section of the country. Our Colonel dispatched a squadron of cavalry, under command of our Major, who advanced as far as Curratuck Court House, and found the General with five hundred troops, ready to march toward our camp, having sent the other portion of his brigade by different routes to Norfolk, with their contrabands and spoils.

He arrived at our camp about midnight, with a train of seventy wagons and carts, of all descriptions. The moon shone brightly as they passed; every vehicle had from three to six negroes of different sizes; it reminded me of the story I had read of Moses' flight out of Egypt, they bringing their masters' mules, oxen and carts with them. They bivouaced in a wood near by. The weather was quite cold. We made the children as comfortable as our means would allow. I surrendered a part of my quarters to the women who had small babes.

General Wilde and staff were our guests during their stay. We gave them a backwoods supper, which consisted of coffee, bear meat and potatoes; they had lain by their camp fires for the last two weeks, and were much fatigued. The General is a tall, slender man, with one arm, the other having been shot off at the battle of Antietam; he is a thorough Anti-Slavery man, and is proud of his command. At Indian Town, North Carolina, he had a fight with a large band of guerillas, killing and wounding many of them; he hung one of them to the limbs of a tree, and burned their camps, many of which he found back from the road, in swamps, and had to march his men single file over fallen trees to reach them. One of his men was captured, and he took the wife of a Lieutenant of the band as a hostage for his safe delivery, declaring she should meet the same fate. The ammunition that was found was marked "Birmingham, Eng." This shows British neutrality, with a vengeance.

The shortest days of the year are now with us, bringing long dreary nights. Our pickets are again firing. I took my gun and went out with a party, and found they had shot a poor negro woman, who, from fear of being captured, had run away from home and her little ones, and through her ignorance, not halting when demanded by the sentinel, received her death wound. Her husband and a number of other plantation hands had been run over the lines during the day by emissaries of the Confederate Government. The poor woman was brought to camp, and soon afterward died. During the night her husband escaped and came into camp, where he found his dead wife. This was for the love of freedom.

> " Yet it may be more lofty courage dwells
>   In one weak heart which braves an adverse fate,
> Than his whose ardent soul indignant swells,
>   W⬛hed for the fight, or cheered through high debate."

The next day a party of soldiers were sent to the place where those negroes lived. Off in the woods was found a guerilla rendezvous. They burned all the buildings, leaving it a scene of desolation.

Old Year's day has arrived, and the scenes around us, which we lately beheld, have assumed a new and chilly aspect. The trees are shorn of their foliage; the fields have lost their verdure, and the wild shrubbery yields no perfume.   Autumn, like a friend in adversity, is now forsaking us; everything around looks dead, and the sweet song of birds will not be heard again till spring time returns.

Winter has its pleasures, even in camp.   The boys congregate around their camp fires, and tell their youthful stories, their past pleasures, and their antici-pations for the future.   The long and tedious marches are abandoned, and winter quarters taken, in place of bivouacing in open fields, or woody glens.

Although the life of a soldier is one of toil, hard-ship and privation, still there is a charm in it that influences all of an enthusiastic or daring disposition. When the soldier is exhausted by fatiguing marches, or overcome by the heat of a Southern sun, he may at times sigh for a return to a life of ease, and long for the quietness of home, and its domestic comforts; but when the joys of meeting friends, and visiting old familiar haunts, are over, he again wishes to return to the exciting scenes of the soldiers life in the field.   To-day we have had a proof of this, in our own camp, as over one half of our veteran men have re-enlisted for the war.

It has been remarked that war unfits men for peace, and anxious fears are entertained that it will be impossible for our armies in the field to lead peaceful lives, after this great struggle is over. I have no fears as to such a result, although they dare face the enemy's cannon, and the rattle of musketry, still they are humane and law abiding citizens, whose sympathies are easily excited, even to tears. Such are the true qualities of a noble and daring heart. Then who would not be a soldier? especially when engaged in such a grand and righteous cause.

I have just visited the pickets on the distant outposts. Along a lonely and scarcely beaten path I walked. Not a murmur was heard. The gray clouds had deepened into night; the pale moon had not yet risen from her accustomed repose to light my footsteps. On my return I am challenged by our pickets at the river side. A voice is heard to say: "Who comes there?" "A friend with the countersign," is the reply. The command is to halt, and advance one step, while the sentinel receives it from you, with the bayonet at your breast; this is the routine, with either friend or foe.

The midnight alarm often brings the soldier from his happy repose; but he is ever ready and willing to meet the foe of his country. He is often sent through the country far beyond the picket and videt posts, to watch the movements of the enemy, through drenching rains and chilly winds, night after night, having no shelter except that which nature affords, with his gun secured under his arm; here in solitude he whiles away many a tedious night, while the stars are kindly smiling, and the flowers are weeping tears of dew; then his thoughts are roaming, thinking of by-gones, still there are griefs in his bosom he cannot quell; no heart near beating in sympathy with his, and no kiss greets him with morning dawn; but hope springs up in his heart that a message will come from some dear loved one, to revive his almost drooping spirit. Homesickness creeps on, as he watches day by day for these comforters of his lonely heart, he becomes discouraged oftentimes, and then deserts; men call him a coward, when he is only starving for sympathy. We should deal kindly with such, for each heart has its own sorrows, which earth cannot always dispel.

1 8 6 4.

THE 1st of January is with us. Here we are pent up in our canvas houses, shivering before our little fire, giving us ample time to reflect on the events of the past year, and the great uncertainty of the future. It is a lovely morning; the sun in its majestic splendor has left the horizon, and is climbing the imaginable arc overhead; the air is piercing cold, instinctively bringing us near the burning embers. The river near by is frozen over, the ice looking like polished glass on which the boys are sporting.

This is New Year's morning, but I can scarcely realize it, here in the backwoods of Virginia; but when I hear the greeting of "Happy New Year," I am reminded of by-gone pleasures and unalloyed happiness which I enjoyed beneath the paternal roof.

War has deprived us all here of the pleasant associations which so often greeted us on the happy New Year's morning.

Our respective friends might all enjoy a visit here to-day, to see our camp, and the comforts of camp life near this great Dismal Swamp, if there are any. The tents are neatly arranged on the streets, and mounted on log cabins, with doors on the street front, and chimneys on the rear, built with barrels, towering high, for flues, with the smoke from them curling upwards.

As you enter a dwelling so rudely constructed, and inquiringly scrutinize the interior, a couch mounted on poles attracts your attention, and perhaps on it lies a lazy inmate; he may be smoking, or engaged in social amusement, having a game of cribbage or euchre with his comrade, to dispel thoughts of home.

In one corner stands his faithful musket, from which has issued many a deadly missile, aimed at the heart of traitors; in another corner stands a rustic rack, whereon hangs a canteen, towel, haversack and looking glass; also a pipe and tobacco in a pouch near by. Under the couch you may see a box of hard tack and a piece of pork, with the grease running from it, all ready prepared, for a march.

With all these camp comforts the soldiers' winter quarters are dreary and monotonous; and nothing is so inspiring as a good social letter, especially from the "family." Newspapers are always welcome, and are eagerly sought for by the soldiers, and read, even to the advertisements, with an interest little dreamed of by the kind friends at home, who send them.

This morning a party of fifty men went out on a guerilla hunt; when near Indian Creek Bridge, they saw off in the woods an old building, which was said to be a guerilla rendezvous. They cleared the house of its inmates, and set fire to it, also the outbuildings, laying them all in ashes; in a stack of corn fodder near by was found a double barreled gun, loaded with shot and ball, which, no doubt, was hid there for use against the Yankees.

This afternoon our veteran recruits were sworn in for another three years; they are to receive a bounty of eight hundred and seventy-five dollars. Everything is quiet in camp, with the exception of occasional firing on our pickets, and it is rumored that the enemy are advancing on us, by way of South Mills.

February is very mild and pleasant thus far. To-day we commemorated the birthday of WASHINGTON, and to-night we have received an order from Major General Butler to report to our Governor, at Albany, New York, for the purpose of enjoying a furlough of thirty days in our native State. This brings joy to many an old soldier, some of whom have not seen their families in over two years, and they are almost wild with delight at the prospect of a speedy reunion with friends at home.

This morning, the 23d of February, we take up our line of march for Norfolk. At sundown the regiment bivouaced near Great Bridge, and resumed their march in the morning, arriving at the defences of Norfolk late in the afternoon, where they bivouaced in the fields two nights, awaiting the arrival of transports from New York.

On the 27th, our whole brigade embarked on board transports, the Eighty-First on board the Prometheus, the Ninety-Sixth on the Cambria, and the Ninety-Eighth on the New Jersey.

It was noon when we weighed anchor and set sail for Hampton Roads. At sundown we cast anchor off Fortress Monroe; a heavy sea was setting in and we dare not venture out that night; it blew a perfect gale during the night. Morning's dawn brought a change of wind, and at sunrise we set sail for the briny deep. We soon rounded Cape Charles, bound northward. The next morning we found we were off Jersey shore, passing Cape May with her monstrous hotels in the distance. This is a great resort for Northerners during the summer months. The highlands of New Jersey are beautiful, standing up boldly from the ocean bed, as if to defy the rolling billows, as they come beating against them.

Away off in the distance is seen Neversink, one of the finest elevations in America, with its peaks towering to the sky, and on its summit stands a beautiful lighthouse, throwing its rays of fire off on the briny ocean, giving the mariner light to avoid the shallow waters, where thousands have been wrecked, and many lost, never to tell their fate.

The sea became calm as our vessel neared the main land, giving us a delightful view of the beautiful scenery which presents itself on either shore, as we sail up the channel which brings the traveler to the great Emporium of America. As we sail up we see the defences of New York and its surroundings, which are immense fortifications of stonework and earth, on which are mounted not less than three hundred guns, some of which are of the largest caliber.

We anchored off Castle Garden; the sun was at its meridian; the waters were quiet, without a ripple on their surface; the sky as beautiful as was ever seen from Oriental shore. This was the last day of winter, but one of the lovliest of the year.

Our Colonel, Adjutant, and myself, went ashore in a small boat, and reported to the commanding officer of the Department.

The next day, which was the 1st of March, our troops disembarked, and proceeded to the Park barracks, where they found good quarters for two days, and in the meantime were reviewed by the Mayor and Common Council, in front of the City Hall; from there we were escorted to Union Square, by the Eighth and Thirty-Seventh New York National Guard, and were again reviewed, by General Burnside; after which the brigade marched to the National Armory, and partook of a collation; from thence we marched to the Hudson River Railroad and took the cars for Albany, arriving there the next morning.

On the following day we were reviewed by the Governor and Legislature, and addressed by Speaker Alvord, in fitting terms. In the evening the regiment took the cars for Oswego, where we were received the following afternoon, in a most sumptuous manner by the citizens of that loyal city.

The day had been wet and exceedingly unpleasant, but our arrival brought out an immense crowd, which filled the streets; although exposed to a drizzling rain,

they were eager to catch a glimpse of the returned
veterans. We were received amid the cheers of the
multitude. The merry pealing of the bells, and roar
of cannon told our welcome. We were escorted to
Babcock's Block, by the National Guards and the
several fire companies of the city, from the balcony
of which we were welcomed in behalf of the civil
authorities, by Mayor Grant, as follows:

Officers and Soldiers:

As the executive officer of this city, I have been
requested to congratulate you on your safe return to
your homes, and to extend to you that cordial welcome which a grateful and generous people are ever
ready to bestow on the brave defenders of their rights,
and the liberties of their country.

To me, personally, it is a great pleasure to be the
medium of communicating the high appreciation of
your townsmen and fellow citizens, of your heroic
deeds, your gallantry, and noble bearing as soldiers.
You came not unheralded; you have not been forgotten
while absent; the eyes of your immediate friends and
fellow citizens have been upon you. Already have
they watched you, and deeply have they sympathized
with you in your long and fatiguing marches, your

exposure and self denial, your patient endurance of the hardships, perils and deprivations of a soldier's life, as well as the determined spirit and unflinching bravery exhibited on the battle field, in the midst of death, carnage, and the war of artillery; when your brave fellows and compatriots were falling around you like the ripe grain before the sickle.

We are happy to greet and welcome you beneath these gloriously dilapidated flags of the noble Eighty-First. If they are tattered and torn, pierced and blood stained, they have never been soiled by the unhallowed hands of the enemy. Under these flags fell the gallant McAmbly. Most nobly have you sustained and bravely defended them; we are proud of you, and honor and respect you.

Officers and soldiers, your record is a glorious one, that of participating in the attack, bombardment and capture of Yorktown, in the bloody battle of Williamsburgh, in the fatigue and inevitable hardships of the camp, the march, and battles of the Peninsula, in the unavoidable exposure, and intense suffering in the swamps of the Chickahominy, in valiantly and successfully sustaining the attack and holding the position against a vastly superior force of the enemy for three and a half hours, in the unequal yet glorious encounter of Fair Oaks, in which heroic and sanguinary battle about eighteen hundred of your brave comrades were slain or wounded, out of five thousand.

In the terrible and glorious seven days fight of that memorable and skillful retreat to James river, you occupying the rear position in that successful movement, your embarkation for South Carolina, and your trip to the Dismal Swamp, are all convincing proofs as to your loyalty to your country.

Amid the hilarity and the convivial congratulations of this proud and glorious day, is to be seen the evidences of real sadness interspersed among this assembly; the mournful eye beholds the remnant of this once full but now decimated regiment with feelings of sorrow and affliction, with the only consoling reflection that the slain valiantly sacrificed their lives in behalf of their country's cause. Their return we cannot welcome, but their daring deeds, their patriotic devotion to their country, its Constitution and laws, and to the good old Union under which we have become so popular and powerful a people, are engraven in letters of living light upon the hearts of their countrymen, and their memory will be hallowed by future generations. It has been your fortune to escape the terrible fate which befel so many of your comrades, and once more to visit your homes, and again embrace the dear ones who have so anxiously and constantly awaited your return.

The exhibition of public respect and feeling manifested by this large gathering of your fellow citizens, who have come together to do you honor, is a flattering testimonial of their confidence and high regard for you. The noble cause in which you are engaged has had much to do in rousing up and bringing forth this demonstration of public sentiment.

A great outrage had been perpetrated on the flag and liberties of our country. The execrable and intolerable dogma of the right of secession of municipalities was proclaimed, the Union was separated, the Constitution entirely disregarded, and the laws set at defiance; treason raised her hydra-head, open rebellion announced, and civil war with all its horrors was inaugurated. The country called for troops and, to your honor will it ever be credited, you answered promptly, and voluntarily offered your lives upon your country's altar, and for the preservation of her liberties.

The people deem it to be a duty, as it is a pleasure, thus to give a befitting reception to their brave defenders. This duty we shall ever be happy to perform as long as there is an absent soldier to return; and our joy and gratitude at your return is only marred by the recollection of the absent faces left behind. Well has the Poet said:

> " Princes and Lords may flourish, or may fade,
> A breath can make them, as a breath has made,
> But a brave soldier is his country's pride,
> Once destroyed can never be supplied."

About three years ago a wicked and gigantic rebellion was projected and inaugurated, to sever and destroy this then happy and glorious Republic. Our laws were violated, our shipping, our forts, our munitions of war, and our revenues, were seized by the ruthless hands of misguided men, in open acts of sedition and conspiracy. Even our noble flag, the priceless legacy handed down to us by our illustrous ancestors, was most insultingly fired upon. A civil and vindictive war being thus instigated, you, with others, most nobly offered your services, your lives, your all, in your country's cause. Your achievements, your heroism, your perils in war, your comrades fallen on the battle field, all, all will be recorded in the history of your country, and the glorious Eighty-First will live on the historic pages, when those here assembled shall be no more.

The country has again called for troops. Your friends and fellow citizens, knowing your gallantry, and lofty devotion to your country and to the cause so dear to your hearts, have solicited a renewal of your services, in these times of imminent peril, relying confidently upon your cheerful acquiescence in the demand and wants of your Government.

Noble and veteran warriors! correctly did they judge that you possessed the patriotism, courage and indomitable spirit of our Revolutionary sires; that you would again volunteer to participate in the hardships, perils, toils and bloody conflicts necessary to quell this rebellion For this purpose you have cheerfully re-enlisted for three years more. For this great sacrifice and devotion to the rights and interests of your country we cannot repay the debt of gratitude we owe you, by any act of ours.

With joy and pleasure do the multitude here assembled hail and congratulate your return. If your return has produced this delight and raised this sentiment of public respect, with what real, heartfelt gratitude and enthusiasm will your fellow citizens receive the intelligence that your patriotism has prompted you again to volunteer, and to re-enter upon this terrible strife, and see it through to the bitter end.

Officers and soldiers, for this great sacrifice of yours, as well as for your former achievements, you have our thanks, our unfeigned gratitude; our most ardent desire and sincere wish is that your future career may be as prosperous and successful as the undertaking is praiseworthy and glorious. May success attend you in every effort; may the fortunes of war be with you in every undertaking, and may all of you live to return again to your friends, after having conquered a peace, quelled the rebellion, restored the Union, maintained the Constitution, and vindicated the outraged laws.

You have enlisted in a glorious cause; in it you have our ardent desires for a successful and triumphant termination. May your movements be guided by wise counsels, and your progress be onward, and forward, until the last rebel is forced to lay down his arms, sue for mercy, and ask for an honorable peace.

Finally, in the name, and also in behalf of your numerous friends, and of all such as are dear to you, I bid you a most hearty welcome.

The Mayor's adddress was received by the boys with enthusiastic cheers.

Our Colonel, in behalf of the regiment responded as follows:

Mr. Mayor, Members of the Common Council and Citizens of Oswego:

Allow me, in behalf of the gallant Eighty-First New York State Volunteers, to tender you a soldier's thanks for the spontaneous outburst of warm hearted feeling manifested by this enthusiastic reception, by the masses of this goodly city. If the people of Oswego are satisfied with our course, we feel amply repaid for all our sacrifices and sufferings. In making and enduring them, we feel that we have only done our duty to our country in this her hour of peril; and, sir, we have not only done all that has been asked of us, but we have, after carefully canvassing the matter, determined to return to the field and do all we can for three years to come, if needed.

Allow me, sir, to refer to the time when those tattered and worn colors that now adorn the platform on which you stand, were presented in yonder park. Two years have elapsed, yet the sentiments of the Hon. Mr. Fitzhugh, uttered on that occasion, are still ringing in our ears: "Go boys, go, and sustain the glorious Stars and Stripes, just presented to you, and you not only, but your children will bless the day, and feel proud when they remember that their fathers helped to crush out the great rebellion of 1861." That sentence, sir, will continue to prompt us to action, and if we, like others that have left before us, should not return at the next return of the Eighty-First, you will do us honor by saying, that by our blood was our nation brought to life. Again let us thank you for this kind reception.

Cheer upon cheer was given for the Eighty-First by the surrounding multitude, and responded to by the boys, when they marched to Doolittle Hall. Here the ladies of Oswego had been busy during the day, preparing a. banquet for the veterans which was a grand affair.

The hall was decorated with flags, and while the veterans were partaking of the good things which the table afforded, the band discoursed delightful music, and the ladies made themselves attentive in waiting on the care worn soldiers, many of whom were the wives, daughters and sisters of these men. After the cloth was removed, speeches were made by a number of the officers, complimenting the ladies of Oswego for their kind reception, and telling them how anxious they were to return and receive their smiles and best wishes. It was midnight before all the audience left, yet the tables were well supplied with refreshments.

The following day our men were furloughed for thirty days, to visit their respective homes, while the officers were detailed on recruiting service, all of whom were to report at Fort Ontario, on the 1st of April.

Our regiment rendezvoused at Fort Ontario, from the 1st to the 12th of April, and then left by rail for Albany, arriving there the next morning, and at night took the steamer St. John for New York. On our arrival there we proceeded to the Park Barracks, where we remained two days, and then embarked on board the transport Ericson, for Fortress Monroe, where we arrived on Sunday evening after a delightful voyage of forty-eight hours.

We lay at anchor until morning, when we were ordered to Yorktown with our whole brigade. I was ordered to Northwest Landing, our old camp, for a detachment of our regiment, and our camp equippage. I left Norfolk at midnight, on horseback, for our camp, arriving there at daylight, having had a very lonely ride, sleeping part of the time on my horse, that faithful animal, who brought me through in safety.

The troops, and seven loads of baggage, started for Great Bridge; myself and detail awaited the return of the teams, with seven others, which were to be sent me by the way of Deep Creek, from Portsmouth. The next morning we left our winter quarters, with thirteen loads, direct for Norfolk, arriving there at sundown. At midnight we were all on board the steamer Webster, bound for Yorktown, where we arrived the following morning, and the old members of the Eighty-First were united with the re-enlisted veterans, who were encamped on the plain, just outside of the fortifications, nearly on the same spot which we had occupied after the retreat from Harrison's Landing, in August, 1862.

It is the last of April, and the weather is quite mild. We have received orders to send all our luggage to Norfolk, except so much as can be put in a small valise, which each officer will be allowed transportation for, during our active spring campaign. The 18th Army Corps is rendezvoused at this place, at Gloucester Point. On the opposite side of the river lays the 10th Army Corps, which has just arrived from the Department of the South, where they have been for the last year hammering at the gates of Charleston, and reducing Fort Sumter.

The entire force is commanded by Major General B. F. Butler, who is a particular friend of Jefferson Davis and the Southern ladies. I hope he may be privileged soon to issue some of his New Orleans orders in the city of Richmond, where they are so much needed; also to release our prisoners from Libby and Belle Isle, who are now starving. The Thirty-Eighth Pennsylvania passed through our camp, having a tame bear with them, weighing about three hundred pounds; it is kept by the boys as a pet, and has been with them ever since the regiment took the field.

This is a beautiful May day. The sun is high in the heavens, throwing its genial rays over hill and plain. The cold winds have ceased to blow, and quiet spring has returned again with her verdant fields and balmy air. The fruit trees are all in blow; the buds which have been so long concealed, have burst forth from their winter prison, giving joy to every eye.

Just two years ago to-day Yorktown was evacuated by the rebel army, under General Magruder, and our forces under General McClellan, entered it triumphantly, planting our flag on the ramparts, which has floated there ever since.

We leave Yorktown to-day, which is the 4th of May, on board of transports; our destination is yet unknown. It is a grand sight to see so many transports, loaded with troops, and the Stars and Stripes floating from so many mastheads. During the night we anchored off Fortress Monroe, and in the morning our transport, John A. Warner, set her bow up the James river.

The sun rose beautiful, and a more splendid May morning I have never beheld. Not less than seventy-five transports, of various sizes, accompanied the expedition, with probably not less than thirty-five thousand men on board.

The James river is wide and deep; its banks are high and well studded with wood. Occasionally is seen a country residence through the thick foliage. This is one of the finest rivers in America, and with Northern enterprize could be made to compare favorably with the Hudson, in point of commerce, but not in variety of scenery.

A portion of our troops are disembarking at Fort Pochahontas, on the east side. Here lay the far-famed rebel craft, Atlanta, which was taken by our gunboats at the mouth of Savannah river. She is a splendid ironclad, carrying eight guns, with an iron cased roof over them.

We reached Bermuda Hundred at sundown. The troops were hastily landed, and our regiment marched out about a mile, and bivouaced in a wheat field for the night. I sought shelter with my horse under a holly tree. Here lay together for the night all our field and staff officers, with their horses by them, with nothing but the earth to rest upon. We flanked ourselves with rails from a fence near by, to prevent the passing troops from running over us. Revielle was sounded, and orders given us to march in fifteen minutes, in which time we had to boil our coffee, and eat our pork and hard tack.

Soon our Corps was on the march for the Petersburg and Richmond Railroad, which lay within ten miles of us. Our regiment marched about six miles, and encamped. About two o'clock heavy firing commenced on our front. The Colonel, Adjutant and myself went forward. On our way we met General Butler and staff; we saluted him, which compliment was returned by the General, who stopped a few minutes for conversation, and informed us that the troops on our right had carried an elevated point, near the railroad, which was an important position. The day was very warm, but our troops were in fine spirits, and felt confident of holding their ground.

This morning, May 9th, we received orders to be ready at daylight, with one day's rations and sixty rounds of ammunition. At sunrise the whole army commenced to move. During the afternoon sharp firing was heard on the right and left; at midnight our left wing was attacked by the Twenty-Fifth South Carolina regiment. They engaged the Twenty-Fifth Massachusetts, who drove them back with the point of their bayonets, with great slaughter. I saw the dead lay in heaps on the field. After the fight I took a walk along the railroad, and found the Third Brigade bending the rails and burning the ties. I went through the woods about a mile, and came upon a turnpike, which led to Richmond; this is the best road I have seen in the South.

Some very heavy firing commenced on the right of our line, which caused our left to be drawn in. We built a barricade across the railroad, to prevent the rebels seeing us withdraw our force, which was done in good order, leaving General Beauregard without an enemy in his front, and returned to our entrenchments. Many fell out by the wayside, exhausted and overcome with the heat. The woods were on fire, spreading over an immense territory, destroying everything in its way.

We are again ordered to march at daylight. Beauregard has left Violet Station, where our last battle was fought, and has taken his troops to Richmond.

Our forces are on his heels, driving him at double-quick, and we are already within nine miles of the rebel capital. We have succeeded in taking the first line of rifle pits, and our right is within two miles of Fort Darling.

It has been raining for four days, and our troops have lain in the trenches all this time, under fire of the enemy, with very little to eat. Our greatest want at present is vegetables. Symptoms of scurvy are now prevalent, and many of us have sore mouths. Our rations for the last ten days have been hard tack, salt pork and coffee. This kind of diet, and lying on the damp earth at night, is rather unwholesome, but we can do no better at present; we must bear our privations patiently, for a soldier has no right to complain, when the Government is doing the best it can.

I have returned to camp. It is the solemn hour of night; the wasting moon sheds a hallowed light upon the earth, and the stars but faintly gleam in their far distant homes. The lone sentinels pace their beats with a firm step; fear is a stranger to their breasts, nor do fancies of unseen danger fill their thoughts, for their visions are on home, and those dear loved ones who are waiting around the old hearthstones for their return.

In the distance the plain is dotted with tents; the camp fires have ceased to burn; within the tent the soldier sleeps, dreaming not of battle fields, nor of scenes of sorrow, but of happy faces and happy days, which makes his sleep so refreshing.

A deep and hollow rumbling comes wafted by the night winds, from the far end of the lines, while the echo sounds far over the plains and through deep ravines. It is the long roll—the cry of "To arms!" Next comes the cry of "Fall in! fall in!" ringing through the camp. The men obey the summons, and prepare for battle; some may tremble and turn pale, but not a word is spoken. Shadows of loved ones and home flit across their memory in quick succession. They are on the eve of battle, and they know it. Who of them will not return? With hearts stout and brave, they march silently to the conflict. Such are the scenes presented to the soldier's mind when on the eve of battle.

The morning dawn brought on a general engagement, on the right of our line, near Drury's Bluff, or Fort Darling, which soon extended along the lines, and lasted until nightfall. Many a brave man fell that day, while battling for his country. Our boys stood their ground nobly. The enemy, with their thirty thousand reinforcements from Richmond, could not drive our troops from the position which they had taken in front of the rebel works.

As the declining sun was throwing its last rays on the bloody battle field, we received orders to fall back to our entrenchments. Our regiment was the last to leave the ground, which was done under the cover of night. Ere midnight our dead were buried, our wounded were all cared for, and our troops once more secure within the fortifications, between the Appomattox and James rivers. Our loss that day did not exceed three thousand men in killed, wounded and missing.

"In fame's eternal camping ground,
Their silent tents are spread,
And glory guards with solemn tread
The bivouac of the dead."

The battle of Drury's Bluff will be long remembered and talked of around the hearthstone of many families both North and South.

This morning, at one o'clock, we were aroused from our sleepy couch by heavy musketry, very near our camp, which proved that the rebels were advancing on us. After about twenty minutes firing, they fell

back, and at daylight renewed their fire with increased
vigor, until sundown. They were met by our troops
with a coolness seldom witnessed. At night our whole
brigade commenced strengthening their works, and
slashing timber in front of them, forming an abattis.
At daylight the rebels sent their shot and shell whizzing over us like hail. The night being foggy, they
succeeded in planting some batteries on our flanks, and
within a thousand yards of our works. I heard balls
from their sharpshooters whiz over my head distinctly.

The rain has commenced pouring down again.
The sick call is beating, and not less than two-thirds
of the regiment are excused from duty, on account of
sickness, and exhaustion.

I have just visited Point of Rocks. On this high
cliff stands a sturdy oak, whose leaves have fallen from
its boughs for more than two centuries, and under
whose shade tradition says Pochahontas saved the life
of Captain Smith, when her father, Powhattan, was
about to sacrifice him to gratify his savage band.

A most delightful view is seen from this rock of the
Appomattox, as it winds its way through the high
bluffs which skirt it on either shore. Its bed is interspersed with islands covered with dense foliage, which
presents a very picturesque appearance. In the far

distance is seen Petersburg, quietly nestling among the highlands of the Appomattox, with her spires pointing heavenward, and the smoke of her factories hanging like mist around her dwellings.

Here is also a fine old farm house, formerly the residence of an F. F V.; at present Uncle Sam occupies it for a hospital. The former occupant left it suddenly, on our arrival here; no doubt thinking Secesh air would be more congenial to his feelings. An ice house was found here, well filled with that article, which was much needed for the sick and wounded soldiers, which at this time was a God-send to us. This ice was made in the winter; it was taken from the river and put together in layers, and then frozen, which made good solid ice.

On my return I rode along the lines of our earth-works, to the James river, and suddenly came upon a group of officers sitting on its banks. I learned it was General Butler and staff, watching the movements of the enemy, who were trying to erect some batteries on the opposite shore.

In the river just beneath our feet, lay several iron-clads, which occasionally threw a shell at the enemy. On the opposite side I saw beautiful wheat fields, and a delightful country; the ravages of war had not

yet visited it. On my return the rebels had commenced an attack on our front. My horse had taken
the wrong road, which brought me near their shell
and shot, at one time they flew thick and fast around
me, sometimes striking too close to be pleasant.

The 20th has already arrived, and to-day we had
quite a severe battle; the left wing of the 10th Army
Corps were engaged near our camp. It commenced
at midnight, and lasted until four o'clock in the afternoon, when the enemy fell back. At night they drove
in our pickets, and commenced a general attack; the
roar of artillery was immense on both sides. It was
a grand spectacle by moonlight. One of our shells
struck a caisson, and up it went, like a volcanic explo-
sion, spreading destruction all around. A grand hurrah went up all along the lines. We soon silenced
their guns, and all was quiet again. At daylight the
enemy sent in a flag of truce, asking permisson to bury
their dead.

This morning, May 27th, we received orders to
strike our tents. In less than an hour our whole
corps was on the move. It is a grand sight to see the
moving columns in the field, and always brings joy to
the soldier; but this is not all that goes to make up
the life of the soldiers who compose the grand army

of the Union. Every soldier on the march is literally a moving kitchen, for he carries his bed and tent, and all that belongs to the culinary department, upon his back; hence, whenever a soldier halts, he is at home, and can proceed to housekeeping at once.

We marched toward the James river, passing through a dense woods and swamp, where we found a corduroy road had been built for us by our Engineer Corps. These roads are formed by first filling in with brush, and then laying timber down for sleepers, or string pieces, after which they are covered with small logs, laid parallel with each other, which are also covered over with earth. In this manner army roads are built through swamps and low, moist ground, enabling the heaviest wagons and artillery to pass over as easily as on our best Macadamized roads.

After a march of three miles through the woods, we came into an open field, where we remained two days; from thence we marched to Bermuda Hundred, and embarked on board transports, bound for West Point, on the York river.

The day is beautiful. The trees which stud the banks of these noble streams are fully leaved. As the sun was sinking in the western sky, throwing a halo of light over the waters of the Chesapeake, we passed Old

Point, bound up York river. The night was pleasant, and, without the least obstruction to impede our progress as we forced our way through the deep waters, early the next morning we arrived at West Point, which lays at the intersection of the Pamunky and Mattapony rivers.

We made our way up the Pamunky in haste, which, by the way, is clearly one of the most crooked rivers in America, and is formed by the waters of the North and South Anna. The Mattapony is formed from the the waters of the Matt, Ta, Po and Ny.

Early in the afternoon we arrived at the White House. This is a place of great note, and has been known by the name of White House since the Revolution. It is one of the sacred spots of Virginia. The Custis family owned this plantation, which comprised many hundred acres.

At this house Gen. Washington courted and married Mrs. Martha Custis. The trees under whose shades they have often wandered are still alive, and in full vigor, forming now a delightful shade for our sick and wounded soldiers. The house was formerly a wooden building, with brick foundation. At present nothing remains but the chimney and foundation, it having been burned since the breaking out of the rebellion.

The property is now owned by General Fitzhugh Lee, of the rebel army, and its occupancy by the military is not materially improving its condition.

This is the last day of Spring, and we have commenced our march towards Richmond. We reached New Castle about midnight, where we bivouaced.

This morning, which is the 1st of June, we received orders to march to Gaines' Mills, which we reached about five o'clock in the afternoon. The day was very warm, and the road very dusty; many fell by the roadside, exhausted by heat and fatigue. We were ordered at once to the front, where the enemy lay awaiting us, behind their entrenchments, at a place called Cold Harbor. Soon the shot and shell commenced flying, as well as railroad iron. The 6th Corps engaged the enemy, and the fighting lasted until near midnight; in the meantime a number of other corps were arriving.

After the fighting ceased my Sergeant and myself laid down to sleep on the battle field, among the dead and dying. We were very much exhausted, and could find but little rest; the earth was cold and damp. I was compelled to get up during the night and warm myself by the camp fire, which was feebly burning;

around it sat some wounded soldiers, who had just been brought in from the picket line. A continual cry for water was heard from the wounded and dying around us; I took my canteen and gave drink to those near by. When morning came, I found many had died, among them were several to whom I had given water but a few hours before. The trenches were already dug by a fatigue party, detailed for that purpose, and before sunrise all the dead were buried, together with the limbs which had been amputated on the previous day.

Early this morning Lieutenant Burke, of our regiment, was killed on the picket line. He was tied up in a shelter tent, with a pole passing through it, which was hung on the shoulders of two boys, and carried to the rear. He was a joival fellow, and often had afforded us much amusement in camp by his histrionic readings, songs and laughable stories.

On the 3d of June a grand charge was made by the 2d, 5th, 6th, 9th and 18th Corps; not less than 125,000 men were engaged. Our Corps, the 18th, made a desperate charge, and carried the works in their front, which made it the most desperate kind of fighting. Night found us in quiet possession of their first line of rifle pits, although repeated charges were made to retake them. All officers were required to be with their respective regiments, and Surgeons within three hundred yards, which brought them under a heavy fire. Our hospital was so near that the enemy's shells passed in and over it, which made it a very unpleasant place for amputating limbs. Our Surgeons worked nobly, looking like so many butchers; many were bareheaded, with sleeves rolled up to their arm pits, some of them spotted all over with blood; they really looked horrifying.

The morning was dark and cloudy, with rain at intervals; the day was cool, and far more favorable for fighting than the hot Wednesday which witnessed our last struggle at Drury's Bluff.

Our regiment made a charge across an open field, and through a dense woods, in which the enemy had a continuous line of rifle pits. The slaughter was terrible; but the works were held with unsurpassed valor. Throughout the day a perfect hail of musket balls and shell were poured in on us, as we lay concealed behind the earthworks. I saw General Grant on the field that day, smoking his cigar as usual, and taking everything with the utmost coolness.

In this engagement our regiment lost fifteen officers and one-half their men. My brother was shot in the foot, in the early part of the engagement. I helped carry him from the field, and had his foot amputated, after which he was sent to the White House. The engagement at Cold Harbor was one of the most severe battles of the campaign. Our loss was not less than twenty thousand killed, wounded and missing. Our Corps lost over five thousand men, and the most of our dead were left unburied on the field.

The body of Captain Ballard was brought from the field with much difficulty, by friends, under cover of night. I took him, Lieutenant Burke and Colonel Weed, of the Ninety-Eighth New York, to the White House, had them embalmed and sent North. The journey with them, at night, was a tedious and dangerous one, carrying them and one other dead officer in an army wagon, without an escort, a distance of seventeen miles through the enemy's country, which was infested by bands of guerillas.

The next morning I returned to the front, in charge of a wagon train, two miles long. About midnight we passed through a deep ravine and swamp, through which a corduroy road had been built. One of the teams, near the rear, got off the road into the swamp and fastened, which delayed us an hour, and we were in danger of being captured. The night previous we had lost eighteen teams near this place, taken by the enemy. It became so dark that we could proceed no further, and we bivouaced for the night in an open field, arriving at the front the next morning shortly after sunrise. I went to the rifle pits where our regiment lay, and delivered a mail.

The rebel sharpshooters kept up a constant firing at us here for twelve days. When the whole army was ordered to the James river, our regiment was sent back to the White House, and took transports for Bermuda Hundred, where we arrived on the 14th and marched to Point of Rocks, bivouaced for the night, and at daylight crossed the Appomattox on a pontoon bridge. After three hours' march, we encountered the enemy, and drove them from the first line of defences of Petersburg, and at sundown stormed and carried the forts which lay within two miles of the doomed city. The charge was made on the first line by the colored troops, who showed no quarter to the foe.

From an elevated line of the captured forts we could see the spires of Petersburg, quite visible, through the foliage of the surrounding timber land. Here and there could be seen little clouds of smoke, bursting suddenly into existence, followed, after several seconds, by the booming of cannon, marking the position of rebel batteries. Most of them were opposite our right wing, and on the other side of the river, farther in the distance, can be seen the clouds of dust arising from the enemy's wagon train.

Yesterday morning, at this hour, the strong breast-works on which I now stand were garrisoned by rebel troops. From here is obtained a splendid view of the surrounding country, spread out like a panorama, with fields, hills and valleys, dotted over with the camps of the two opposing armies, the one commanded by General Grant, the other by General Lee.

It was a good day's work, when we consider the value of the captures and the importance of the position gained; and all the glory is attached to the 18th Army Corps. This achievement, added to the service rendered by this corps at Cold Harbor, for thirteen days, makes our record in conjunction with the Army of the Potomac, truly a brilliant one.

By the present movement on the south side of the James, a new order of operation begins; we not only threaten the communication of the enemy, but we plant ourselves across it, and cut them off from the city of Richmond, which will cause Lee to change his base of operations, or lose the use of the railroads coming into Petersburg from the South.

Returning to the rear to-day, I overtook some soldiers carrying an officer from the •field. They halted a moment to rest, and I inquired of them who they had there. They informed me it was the Major of the One Hundred and Eighteenth New York. I immediately dismounted, as it was my friend and townsman, Major Charles Pruyn, and accompainied his remains to the rear, where he was put in a small outbuilding. On examining his wound, it appeared to be made by a shell or solid shot, carrying away his heart and lungs. I saw a Chaplain, who promised me he would have him embalmed and sent home. I gave him his mother's address, and afterward learned that the promise had been fulfilled.

Only a few days ago I was with him at Cold Harbor, sitting under a tree on the battle field quietly taking a lunch. He was then suffering from the effects of a wound in his foot, from which he had not yet recovered. He seemed full of hope, expecting to be mustered out of the service at the end of the summer campaign. This was the last conversation I had with him. He was a noble fellow and a brave officer, and his loss was deeply felt by his comrades.

The commanding General issued the following congratulatory address :

" *To the Eigthteenth Army Corps:*

"The General commanding desires to express to his command his appreciation of their soldierly qualities, as they have been displayed during the campaign of the last seventeen days.

"Within that time they have been called upon to undergo all the hardships of a soldier's life, and been exposed to all its dangers. Marches under a hot sun have ended in severe battles; after the battles, watchful nights in the trenches taken from the enemy. But the crowning point of the honor they are entitled to has been won since the 13th inst., when a series of earthworks in a most commanding position, and of most formidable strength, have been carried, with all the guns and material of war, of the enemy, including prisoners and colors. The works have all been held, and the trophies remain in our hands. The victory is all the more important to us, as the troops have never been regularly organized in camp, where time has been given them to learn the discipline necessary to a well organized Corps d'Armee. They have been hastily concentrated, and suddenly summoned to take part in the trying campaign for our country's being. Such honors as they have won will remain imperishable.

"To the colored troops comprising the division of General Hinks, the General commanding would call the attention of his command. With the veterans of the 18th Corps they have stormed the works of the enemy and carried them, taking guns, and prisoners, and in the whole affair they have displayed the qualities of good soldiers."

On the 17th of June we were ordered to Point of Rocks. Crossing the Appomattox on pontoons, we arrived there at midnight, and bivouaced in a field, where we remained three days, to obtain a little rest, clothing, and change of food. On the night of the 21st we returned to the entrenchments we had lately left, which were within about one mile of the city of Petersburg.

Pontoon bridges are built by using small boats for butments, anchored in the stream, parallel to each other, a distance of twelve feet apart. These are flat-bottomed, being about four feet wide, thirty feet long, and nearly two feet deep. The string pieces are about three by six inches thick, and the floor plank one inch thick, all of oak, which are secured by pins and ropes. Sometimes straw is put over the bridge floor to prevent the enemy hearing the tread of the troops while crossing. These bridges are very readily constructed by the pontoniers, who have charge of this work. A half a mile can be laid in one night. They are transported on pontoon carriages, drawn by eight horses, through the country, following the army; each boat contains the timbers, floor plank and anchors necessary for a span. This branch of the service is under charge of the Engineer Corps, who have been of great service during the war; their duties have been numerous, arduous and dangerous.

This afternoon we were visited by President Lincoln and General Grant; they passed our lines amid the deafening cheers of the army.

The weather is very dry and hot, and I have pitched my fly in a pine grove, to escape the hot rays of the sun. Here I found a quiet sleep, the first I have had in six weeks.

A general cannonading commenced early this morning, along the line of the rebel earthworks, throwing solid shot and shell into our quarters, which compelled us to leave them, for nearly an hour. One shell exploded over my head, throwing its fragments all around me; another fell among the horses, but did not explode. I picked it up and laid it away for future use. In the meantime the rebels charged on our pickets, driving them in. Our boys were ready to receive them, as they advanced. When the rebels found our fire was too hot for them, they fell down and surrendered themselves up to our brigade. There was some four hundred of them, and about two hundred killed.

I had a conversation with a rebel prisoner, who had lost his leg, and was patiently waiting for our surgeons to opperate on him. He remarked to me that he thought it very strange to meet with our regiment in so many engagements, the places being so remote from each other. He said his regiment had engaged the Eighty-First at Violet Station and at Drury's Bluff, then again at Cold Harbor, and a few days afterward he was taken prisoner by them in front of Petersburg. He said our Corps, the 18th, was called by them the "Flying Corps." Our men were kept in light marching order; they were allowed to carry only a blanket and a half shelter tent with them. Our corps was designed to act with the Army of the Potomac, when necessary, which they did, and, I understood, much to the satisfaction of the Lieutenant General.

After every battle comes saddening sights. If you wish to see the "wrinkled front" of "grim visaged war," visit the hospital after a battle. Go to the operating table and observe the delirium of the subject, as the great finger of the surgeon is exploring his bleeding wound, while the sufferer is under the effects of chloroform, that blessed neutralizer of pain.

Sometimes the subject lies passive under the severest operation; at other times he imagines himself on the battle field, in deadly conflict with his antagonist, and then again singing some favorite song; his physical energies exhausted, he sinks into a short sleep, and on awakening finds his wounds dressed, and oftentimes minus a limb. There are some who sleep that sleep which knows no awakening, gone "to that bourne from which no traveler returns."

Return to the hospital in the morning, by gray twilight, ere the sun has arisen; there you will see the attendants bringing out those who have died during the night, laying them in their blankets, for their winding sheet, some with their martial cloak around them, in a row outside of the hospital, preparatory to their burial. Go count those little headboards, made from cracker boxes, which stand in rows over the graves of the dead. Under yonder tree, perchance, the form of some acquaintance, or soldier friend, whose warm hand, which is now cold in death, you but yesterday grasped, may rest beneath one of those headboards. Virginia is filled with such little mounds, where the dead heroes lie, with nought else to mark their last resting place, or tell the tale, that here lies one who fought and died for his country's cause, which is the cause of mankind.

The cars have commenced running on the road leading from City Point to Petersburg, which will make transportation much easier, both for the wounded and supplies.

I received orders this afternoon, from headquarters, to proceed to Norfolk, for the purpose of bringing our regimental books and papers. I took my horse and orderly and rode to City Point. The day was hot and dry, the road one cloud of dust, which was as fine as flour, and almost suffocated us. At City Point we passed by the quarters of Lieutenant General Grant, which are in a fine old mansion, standing on a high bluff, at the junction of the James and Appomattox rivers, beautifully hemmed in with foliage; at the base of the hill is the new wharf, which had just been finished, with the cars on it, loaded and ready to be drawn to the front. The river was filled with transports, many of which were loaded with troops, who had just arrived to fill our depleted ranks. The sun had just set, and I learned from the Quartermaster at that place, that no boat would leave for Norfolk until morning. This made it necessary to secure lodgings for the night, which I found on board the Sanitary boat, where I had a comfortable bed, and in the morning a good breakfast, which was the best I had eaten in nearly two months.

I took passage on the Highland Light, having a delightful sail down the James river, arriving at Norfolk about six o'clock in the afternoon.

On the 1st of July I returned to Fortress Monroe and took the steamer John A. Warner, for City Point, arriving there at sundown. I obtained a conveyance from the Quartermaster, and started for the front. The night was beautiful, the moonlight beaming from a soft Southern sky, floating through the forest trees, lighting them with a bewitching kind of beauty. The air was balmy, and the sky without a cloud; fireflies sparkling like diamonds in the dense forest were flitting around; the cry of the whippoorwill resounded through the woodlands and along the banks of the river; while the hoarse cry of the croaking toads rose from the marshes.

Soon I heard the booming cannon far in the distance. A little later continuous volleys of musketry were heard, indicating plainly that I was nearing the enemy and our outer lines. Soon after I reached camp much fatigued with my journey.

Independence morning is ushered in by the booming of cannon from our forts far and near, and the bands and drum corps are discoursing beautiful music at the different headquarters along the lines.

Good music is a great accessory to an army. Oftentimes it drowns the groans of the wounded and dying on the battle field. The soldiers perform all their duties by the blast of the bugle or the taps of the drum, and the calls are under charge of the chief musician or Drum Major, who details one drummer from the corps each day to perform the routine duties of the camp calls. First comes Reveille, at sunrise; then the Sick Call, when all the sick assemble at the Surgeon's quarters, where they are examined and, if necessary, excused from duty for the day; next the Sergeants' Call, who assemble at the Adjutant's quarters, and report the number of men in their charge, to him, and also receive special orders; at nine o'clock, Guard Mounting, which is beat on the color line. Officers', Breakfast, Dinner and Supper Calls are also made; then comes the Retreat, at sundown; at nine o'clock the Tattoo, and half an hour later, Taps, peremptorily requiring that all lights to be put out in camp. The most interesting of all calls is the Long Roll, which brings the regiment into line of battle.

Both armies seem to be quiet. Large trains are arriving from City Point, with sanitary stores, such as lemons, oranges, potatoes, cabbage, and, best of all, onions, which we have been so much in need of for the last two months. I think sundown found the entire stock devoured.

For the last two weeks I have been very busily engaged in making out my returns. Having very suddenly been taken ill, with symptoms of a fever, our Surgeon sent me to the field hospital, near Spring Hill. Here I remained nineteen days, gradually failing for want of proper treatment, and over doses of quinine, which the surgeons seem to give for every ailment, from a sore toe to a headache.

On the 24th I was sent to the Chesapeake Hospital, on a steamer, with three hundred others, sick and wounded, arriving there at noon.

It is a beautiful August morning. My window at the Chesapeake Hospital opens on the green and velvety lawn, in the center of which floats our glorious banner, from a high flagstaff. The bleating sheep, the plaintive cry of the sea birds, and the enchanting beauty of ocean, sky and land, all present a scene which Eden itself could hardly have rivaled.

The building is large, and well adapted to hospital purposes, it being used exclusively for officers. Its apartments are well furnished, and the building is well provided with ventilation. One of Ericsson's caloric engines fills the massive tanks near the roof with water, so there is an abundant supply in each story, for bathing and other purposes. The building was originally erected for a young ladies' school, and was used for that purpose until the madness of treason desolated the homes of Virginia.

There are about six hundred patients at present, mostly the sick and wounded from the battle fields of Virginia. They are constantly coming in, as there has been no cessation of hostilities for the last two months. This hospital will accommodate about twelve hundred patients. To the right and left, in the foreground, are barrack hospitals, built in the form of a Greek cross, cottage style, and each will contain about two hundred patients.

When a patient is received at the hospital, he is conducted to his room, At the head of his bed is a card case, and in it a card, on which is written his

*15

name, rank, regiment, and corps; also the place he was sent from, his disease or wound, his age, nativity, and postoffice address. If he dies while here, as many do, he is taken to the end of the hall, in the ward where he lies; at this point a dumb waiter passes from the ground floor to the attic story, on which conveyance he is carried down to the first floor, and from thence, on a litter, to the dead house, where he is embalmed or placed in a coffin and prepared for burial.

Every soldier who dies here, either white or black, is honored with a military funeral. An escort with trailed arms follows him to the grave; the Chaplain performs the burial service, and a volley of musketry from the escort proclaims that the tired soldier sleeps that last sleep from which there is no awakening. A headboard with the name, rank and regiment of the officer painted on it is always carried with the coffin, and placed at the head of the grave.

The mail is received here every morning. The Postmaster makes out a list of the letters to be distributed, and gives them to the master of each ward, who delivers them to the patients, and for all registered letters takes a receipt, which is carefully filed. The same care is exercised in reference to boxes received by express. If the soldier has died, they are returned to those who sent them, as well as all other effects belonging to him, to which business it is the special duty of the Chaplain to attend.

Connected with this hospital there is a farm and garden, consisting of an hundred acres of fertile land. The soil is light and easily cultivated. The farming and gardening afford very amusing and healthful employment for the numerous convalescents. The morning glory and cypress vine thrive here with wonderful luxuriance, putting forth flowers in the greatest profusion. The fences are entirely covered with a dense background of dark green, enlivened with bursting buds of the most brilliant colors. Thus this military farm is appropriately girded with breast-works, ramparts and bastions of gorgeous flowers. In front of the officers' quarters, where the invalids are continually passing, a neat little flower garden is laid out, which is chiefly under the superintending care of our lady nurses.

There is no beam of sunshine so bright as that which flows from the consciousness of a useful life. It is well that flowers should adorn the parterres of such homes; and these flowers will bloom in none the less lovely hues, and will emit no less fragrant odors, because the pale, tottering invalid soldier is charmed

by their beauty, and his senses refreshed by their perfume. Every home should be adorned and beautified
with flowers; they leave a lasting impression, especially
on the minds of the young.

The Surgeon in charge, Dr. McClellan, the head
of this establishment, endowed with energies which
never tire, throws the support of his encouragement,
and the vigilance of his eye, upon every measure to
promote the general good; and he has shown liberal
economy in expending tens of dollars now, that he
may save hundreds in the autumn.

Between two and three thousand bushels of potatoes will be raised here this year, and melons and
squashes by the wagon load. The demand for the hospitals is such that everything must be furnished by
tens and hundreds of bushels.

Early in May last, I am told, the vegetable garden
began to yield its fruits. From that time until the
frosts of December the patient will receive an abundant supply, with the morning dews upon them. The
soil and climate is such, that two crops each year can
be raised on most of the land. The cavalry camps in
the vicinity afford, for the present, an abundant supply
of dressing for the land, which is a great item in the
expense of cultivating a garden.

The Hampton hospitals are near by, just across a small stream which flows into the bay; they form quite a picturesque village, consisting of about thirty cottages. These buildings are so placed as to form a triangle, embracing within its spacious area a lawn of many acres, traversed by walks, and lined by young shade trees. The hand of taste has scattered here and there, beds of blooming shrubbery and flowers. Most of these cottages are called hospital wards, containing fifty beds each. These spacious rooms are open to the ridge, are well warmed, and thoroughly ventilated, at the apex of the roof, and are kept in a perfect state of neatness, which the most accomplished New England housewife cannot excel.

The advantages of the cottage form of wards are manifest; there are no stairs to climb, no impure air to be inhaled by the patients; and in case of fire, the sick and wounded can be instantly removed. There are also many advantages in having the sick together. The soldiers, accustomed to the most social life known upon earth, would be lonely in separate apartments. In the ward they are company for each other, as the vast majority are not seriously ill. There are over two thousand sick and wounded here now; some are sitting up in their beds, reading; others talking or singing, playing chess or some other innocent game, to while away the slowly passing hours of hospital life.

The man who is convalescent, or whose wounds are healing, and who is soon to be discharged, to go home to his friends, is often the happiest of men. The sick man who is recovering, sees a smile in every blade of grass, and hears a song of joy in every whisper of the sea breeze, as it fans his feverish cheek.

Near by is the country seat of the late ex-President, John Tyler; his parlor is now used as a school room for contraband children, where is being conferred the blessings of education upon a race just emerging from barbarism. Also, near by is the beautiful mansion of Senator Mallory, who is now a member of the rebel Congress. His broad acres are confiscated, and are bearing abundant food for the invalid soldier. His residence affords a beautiful home for the Surgeon in charge of these hospitals, who is a man that knows how to appreciate the good things of this world.

There are thousands in our land who have had, and who still have, friends sick and wounded in the hospital. Many a patriotic father has had his heart torn with anguish, as he read the name of his own son in the list of wounded. Many a heroic mother, who girded her son with her own hands, for this most holy war for human rights, cannot sleep at night, as she thinks of her loved boy, bleeding and languishing far away from friends, in the wards of a hospital.

It is indeed a hard lot; and yet how few of these sorrowing ones have any conception of the abounding comforts which our Government has provided for its stricken soldiers; comforts, generally, vastly greater than could be found in many homes.

I am convalescent, and have been anxiously awaiting the reply to my application for a leave of absence, to go North, for the purpose of recruiting my health, by inhaling the cool mountain air, which is so much more invigorating than the miasmatic breeze that sweeps over us here, from the swamps and lowlands of this Peninsula.

The clerk has just notified me that my papers have arrived, and have been approved, which makes me feel almost like another man. Out of one hundred applications but four were approved by General Butler.

I left the Chesapeake Hospital, where I had spent three weeks. I took the horse cars, for the Fortress, which was about a mile and a half distant, winding its way through a wilderness of tents, occupied by happy contrabands. At the Fortress I took the steamer Georgiana for Baltimore. We left near sundown, and proceeded up the bay. The night was dark, with a heavy sea rolling in from the ocean, the boat making the waves look like sheets of fire in our track. We stopped at Point Lookout to put ashore some prisoners, recently taken at Dutch Gap. Morning dawn found our boat nearing Fort McHenry, one of the defences of Baltimore. A little further beyond is seen Federal Hill, which overlooks the city, and is manned by volunteer troops.

The boat landed at the city wharf. I took my breakfast at the Maltby House, and from there took the cars for the Quaker City. At Havre de Grasse the whole train of cars were run on board of a steam ferry boat, carrying us across the river in safety. We then proceeded on our journey, without a change of cars, and arrived at the City of Peace, at noon; we continued our journey, arriving at Jersey City at six o'clock P M. The ferry boat conveyed us across the bay; as we were nearing the shore, the North river boat was just leaving the dock, much to my disappointment, as I had expected to connect with it.

I took the day boat the next morning. It was a beautiful day, and the boat was loaded with passengers, mostly on a pleasure trip. The boat's bow was turned up the river, and left the dock with flying colors.

Hoboken lay just opposite, with her walks shaded with large trees, and extending for nearly two miles along the banks of the Hudson, terminating with the Elysian Fields. This place is noted for its many fine villas and country seats of opulant citizens, which gives the place an air of rural comfort not often met with so near a large city. A little above this, on the same side of the river is Weehawken; it lies near the water's edge, and is severed from the land view by a precipitous ledge of rocks, which give it the privacy usually sought for in such places.

Here it was that General Hamilton fell mortally wounded in a duel with Colonel Burr. There was formerly a monument standing on the spot where he fell, but it has been removed. We soon passed Fort Washington, on the east bank of the river, which was taken by the British in the early part of the Revolution. Opposite this place, upon the brow of the Palisades, is the site of Fort Lee, which was abandoned by our forces. Here the Palisade rocks present, all along on the west margin of the river for many miles, a perpendicular wall, varying from two to five hundred feet in height. These are sometimes covered with brushwood, sometimes capped with stunted trees, and sometimes perfectly bare, but always showing the

16

upright cliff, at the base of which is scarcely room
enough for a foot path. Here and there, in the cleft
of a rock is seen a fisherman's hut, extending to the
very margin of the stream. The water, a very few
feet from the shore is deep, so that vessels run quite
close to its rocky sides.

We passed Spuyten Duyvel and the mouth of Har-
lem river, which forms Manhattan Island. A few
miles further ride brings us to Sunnyside, the beautiful
rural residence of Washington Irving, the great American historian.

Tarrytown is near by, at which place Major Andre
was arrested by those noble patriots, Paulding, Wil-
liams and Van Wart.

We are now nearing Sing Sing, which lays off to
the right, on a quiet bay, with its white buildings,
looking like monuments in the distance. Haverstraw
lies to the left, on the opposite bank of the river, which
is a neat little village. Just above is Stony Point,
the site of a fort during the Revolution; a lighthouse
now crowns the apex.

Peekskill is in sight; it is one of the most romantic
places on the Hudson. On the opposite shore is seen
Dunderburg, or Thunder Mountain. Near by is the
place where Palmer was executed by order of General

Putnam, whose memorable reply to Governor Tryon, who wrote a letter, threatening vengeance if he was executed, deserves an enduring record. It briefly and emphatically unfolds the true character of that distinguished hero. The note ran thus:

"SIR—Nathan Palmer, a Lieutenant in your service was taken in my camp as a spy; he was tried as a spy; he was condemned as a spy; and you may rest assured he shall be hanged as a spy.

"I have the honor to be, yours, &c.,

"ISRAEL PUTNAM."

"P. S. This afternoon he is hanged."

One mile above Peekskill is seen Anthony's Nose. This mountain is a complete mass of rocks; it rises very abruptly from the river, to the height of eleven hundred feet, with the Dunderburg on the opposite shore. Various stories are told concerning the manner in which one of these mountains obtained its name; but little credit can be given to any of them.

We are just turning the steep bluff which brings us, unquestionably, to one of the most romantic places on the Hudson, West Point. Here the mountain towers to the ethereal vault above, making our vessel appear to a spectator on its summit, but a mere skiff. The ascent is very abrupt on all sides, and the surrounding craggy hills seem to be nothing but masses of rocks, fantastically heaped by nature, crowding the stream into a channel less than half a mile in width.

West Point is noted chiefly as the seat of the Military Academy, where most of our regular army officers graduate, receiving a military education at the expense of the Government. Many of the rebel officers were educated here, including Jeff Davis, all of whom have an oath registered to defend the Union and support the Constitution, which they are now basely seeking to destroy. No punishment can be meted out too severe for such perjured villains, when captured. On the river bank near the parade ground is Kosciusko's garden, whither he was accustomed to retire for study and reflection. Near this spot is a clear boiling spring, enclosed in a marble reservoir. Near the landing is the rock from which was stretched across the river a chain, during the Revolution, to prevent vessels ascending the river. Some of the links are preserved as a curiosity; they are near three feet long, made from bars of iron, two inches square.

A few miles above this place is Undercliff, the residence of General George P. Morris, the poet. It is situated on an elevated plateau, rising from the eastern shore of the river, in which he has displayed great taste in the selection of such a commanding and beautiful position. Immediately opposite, rising almost perpendicular from the water, stands the "Old Crow's Nest," one of the most beautiful elevations in America. The following is a description given by Drake:

"'Tis the middle watch of a summer's night—
The earth is dark, but the heavens are bright,
Nought is seen in the vault on high,
But the moon, and stars, and the cloudless sky,
And the flood which rolls its milky hue,
A river of light, on the welkin blue;
The moon looks down on the old Crow's Nest,
She mellows the shade on his shaggy breast,
And seems his huge gray form to throw
In a silver cone on the waves below;
His sides are broken by spots of shade,
By the walnut boughs and the cedars made,
And through their clustering branches dark
Glimmers and dies the firefly's spark,
Like starry twinkle, that momently break
Through the rifts of the gathering tempest rack."

We are approaching Newburgh. Before us lies a beautiful bay, curving to the north, until it is lost in the distance. Sprinkled through the whole course, with the white sails of the numberless vessels that float upon its surface, in the distance, is seen fine cultivated fields, elegant villas, and neat rural cottages, gleaming through the tufts of foliage that surround them.

A short distance south of the village of Newburgh stands the old stone mansion in which General Washington held his headquarters, when the army was encamped here, during the Revolution.

It is noon, and we have made half our journey, which brings us to Poughkeepsie, the first table land along the Hudson, and is seen conspicuously, both in ascending and descending the river.

The gong is sounding for dinner; my journey has given me a ravenous appetite. A grand rush is being made for the saloon below, and my weak knees hardly feel able to stand the pressure of the stronger ones. I have secured a good seat at the head of one of the tables, which is loaded with all the delicacies of the season, and got up in the most approved style. The guests spent an hour in devouring the eatables. When I returned to the deck, the Catskills could be seen through the misty air, far in the distance. We sailed for near an hour before we seemed to near them. Suddenly our boat took another course, following the bend in the river, and soon we were brought in full view of the high peaks, and of the far famed Mountain House, which is one of the coolest places of resort during the summer months, commanding an extended view of the surrounding country.

We are sailing through the deep water, and rounding a point of land which brings us to a high bluff, on which is situated the city of Hudson. Ships can ascend the river as far as this place, which is one hundred and twenty miles from Manhattan Island. Tradition says that Henry Hudson, who was the discoverer of this river, ascended as far as this place, which bears his name. He went on shore in one of the canoes, with an old Indian, who was the chief of forty men and seventeen women, whom he found in a house made of the bark of trees, which were well finished. He saw large quantities of corn and beans, already gathered to dry, beside a great deal more growing in the fields; two mats were spread to sit on, and eatables were brought in red wooden bowls.

Two men went off with their bows and arrows, to kill wild fowl, and soon returned with two pigeons; they also killed a fat dog, and in a very little time skinned it with shells, which they got out of the water. He was invited to stay with them for the night, which invitation he did not accept. When he was ready to return to his ship, the natives concluded he would not stay with them for fear of their bows and arrows, they broke them in pieces and threw them in the fire. He also found grapes, plums, other fruits, and pumpkins, growing here in great abundance.

Two hours sail brought us to the Capital of the Empire State, which presents a most beautiful appearance from the river, being a city built on five hills, with Buttermilk creek, Beaver creek, Fox creek, and Tivoli creek passing down through and under its streets. The State Hall and the Capitol stand on the brow of a hill, some two hundred feet above tide water, from the domes of which a most beautiful view of the river and the surrounding country can be obtained. To the west is seen one vast sandy plain, extending as far as Schenectady, an Indian name, signifying the end of the pine plains.

The picturesque beauty of the Hudson river is beyond description; its banks forming gentle grassy slopes, or covered with forests to the water's edge, or crowned by neat and thriving villages. The legendary and historical interests associated with numerous spots combine to render the Hudson the classical stream of America.

Just two years ago I passed down this beautiful river, under the pale rays of a harvest moon, flushed with health and cheered with the hope that peace would crown our efforts. I left my home, wife and little ones for the privations and dangers of the battle field. It was a subject which had long agitated my mind, and no easy one to decide upon. But my patriotism finally triumphed over my selfishness. I knew the time had come when a great and crushing blow must be dealt, or our country would be lost. My wife did not try to weaken my resolution, but helped fit out my wardrobe for the field.

"The wife who girds her husband's sword,
Mid little ones who weep or wonder,
And bravely speaks the cheering word,
What though her heart be rent asunder,
Doomed nightly in her dreams to hear
The bolts of war around him rattle,
Hath shed as sacred blood as e'er
Was poured upon the plain of battle!"

Now I return from the battle field, sick and weary from the toils of an active campaign, and almost disheartened, even amid victories which have crowned our arms, but as I near home a cheering hope fills my bosom, with thoughts of the old hearthstone and the loved ones around it, who are so anxiously awaiting my return. At sundown I again gazed on the beautiful peaks of the Catskill, which lay off to the south, and I

once more saw the rural cottage in the distance, with
its porch and tower, where the woodbine climbs so
graceful, and hangs in such profusion, with the Stars
and Stripes floating above the battlements, where they
were raised at the commencement of the rebellion. I
see its winding roads and walks, the green lawn, with
its trees, flowers and shrubbery, which makes it a
delightful spot to me, for it is my home:

> "'T is sweet to hear the watch dog's honest bark
> Bay deep mouth'd welcome as we draw near home,
> 'T is sweet to know there is an eye will mark
> Our coming, and look brighter when we come."

The sultry days of August have faded and gone.
The distant hills are bathed in a smoky light as I
view them from Woodbine Cottage. The pure air
from the hills around will help renew my strength,
and I then shall be able to return to my duties in the
field, with renewed hope in the final triumph of our
arms, resulting in a lasting peace.

This is a beautiful September morning; the landscape never looked more lovely. The dewdrops sparkle
in the sun like diamonds, from every leaf where they
had gathered during the night. Fruit and flowers are
in abundance, all producing such a contrast with the
once peaceful and sunny South.

The original term of enlistment of some of our companies has expired. For three long years have they been in the service, and how varied has been the scenes and terrible the conflicts in which they have been engaged. How little do those at home know the suffering that has been endured by these brave soldiers on the battle field, in prisons, and hospitals. Our country should ever be grateful for their services. Many of those brave men had left pleasant homes, expecting to be absent from them only a few months; fears were really entertained by some of them that they would not be required to take part in the great struggle for liberty and human rights; but in this they were disappointed; they have all been called, and hundreds of thousands of others. Many now lie in the cold arms of death; they fill a soldier's grave on some battle field, or in a hospital graveyard.

The conflict still rages with a determination the world has never before witnessed. Success attends the Union armies everywhere, and with such Generals as Grant, Meade, Sherman, Thomas, Sheridan, and others, to lead our gallant soldiers in the field, there can be no such word as fail. The cause in which we fight is just, and when in the providence of God, the rebel hosts shall be dispersed, peace will come again, crowned with liberty to the captive, who has been so long in bondage, and ruled by the iron hand of despotism, which has sought to perpetuate the institution of Slavery at the sacrifice of a Republican Government. The day is breaking and the dark clouds which have mantled our sky are passing away, showing bright gleams of the far away blue.

An overwhelming majority of the votes of a free people will soon declare that the Union candidate for the Presidency, Abraham Lincoln, who has a solemn oath registered in Heaven to preserve and defend the Constitution, is their chosen pilot to conduct the ship of State through the storms which have threatened to destroy her.

The re-election of President Lincoln and the defeat of General George B. McClellan will save our country from everlasting disgrace, thereby rebuking the Chicago Convention, that nest of traitors who were willing to barter the liberties of twenty millions of freemen for the votes of a few Southern slaveholders, also bringing into contempt our grand army of patriots, who are struggling for Constitutional freedom against tyranny, that bitter foe to free institutions and humanity.

The day of jubilee is near at hand. The signs of the times plainly indicate that the rebellion is near its end. Its leaders see there is no hope for the Confederacy. They are quarelling among themselves, and will soon be ready to make the best terms possible to save their necks from the halter, which is now being made from a plant growing on their own soil. The only fear I now have is, that they may escape just punishment through the magnanimity of the best Government the world has ever known.

The occupation of peace men and peace newspapers is gone. Peace is coming from a different direction than that indicated by the prophecies of the peace patriots. It is coming as the legitimate end of a successful war, not as the unhappy result of disgraceful compromise. It is coming with the glorious old flag, not with the white rag of submission to the South, or the Stars and Bars of Southern independence. Soon will be heard the booming of cannon, ringing of bells, and the huzzahs of the people, in one continous echo all through the land, from the St. John river to the Rio Grande, from the rolling billows of the Atlantic to the quiet and peaceful waters of the Pacific, rejoicing for the preservation of our glorious Union and the triumph of our dear old flag.

"Long may it wave,

O'er the land of the free and the home of the brave."

The following letters were written from the army to a friend North, and it is thought may prove interesting to those readers who have gone with us through our Random Sketches and Wandering Thoughts:

CAMP EIGHTY-FIRST REGIMENT, N. Y. VOLS., ⎰
YORKTOWN, VA., September 23, 1862.   ⎱

MY DEAR FRIEND—You will see by the above, our location in the Army of the Potomac. After the retreat from Harrison's Landing, our brigade was sent here to defend this place. The Army of the Potomac has had some hard fighting, and been unfortunate in many respects, still I have not lost confidence in its leader, "Little Mac." Croakers at home and abroad, as well as the weak kneed and feeble, are often discouraged, even in the brightest hour.

I supppose many were frightened when they heard the rebels had crossed into Maryland. I wished they had went on to New York; it would be just the place to have them. I think it would awaken the North to a sense of their duty, for they would then realize what war really is.

Many of the rebels will never see Richmond again. We, of course, must expect to lose many a brave fellow, but that, you know, is the fortune of war. I hope our depleted ranks will soon be filled up, and that the fight will continue until the surrender of the rebel Capital. I think we can stand the loss of men better than they. Constant fighting will conquer them, and finish up the rebellion.

I have great faith in the Government putting down this rebellion. As sure as the sun shines in the east, so sure will this Union be saved, and her free Constitution left unimpaired. These croakers at the North are nothing more than Squaw men, who would abandon their homes and families, through fear, or surrender the Government into the hands of traitors, and become the subjects of a Despotism.

For one, I am satisfied to deprive myself of the comforts of home for the good of my country, and the future advancement of the human race; and they who are not willing to sacrifice anything to preserve the heritage bequeathed to them by their fathers are not worthy the name of American citizens.

Thoughts of home often come to the soldier in camp, with a thousand pleasant memories. He often thinks of the loved ones he has left behind, and may perhaps never again hear their pleasant voices, or see their smiling faces; but these feelings are not to be indulged in by the soldier, for his duties will not permit it; such thoughts almost unfit him for the duties devolving on him; he must drive them from his mind. I find a good antidote for this in the saddle. Each day I take a ride through the country; my horse, "Jim," works well under the saddle, and has been much company to me since I left home; I hardly know how I should while away the monotony of the camp without him.

President Lincoln's proclamation has been issued, freeing all negroes in the States which may be in rebellion on the first of January next. It creates quite a stir in our camp among the officers and men. Some are rejoicing over it, while others are threatening to abandon the service, declaring that they came tó fight for the Union and to maintain the Constitution. They regard the President's policy as a direct infringement of it. I think the "second sober thought" will show them that it will deal the death blow to the rebellion, and without it we cannot succeed in the work we have undertaken. To turn the negro against them will be an element of great strength; fighting them, as it were, with their own weapons.

Our accomodations in camp are poor. We have old shelter tents, which will hardly keep the dew off. A tin cup and plate, a pocket knife and fork, a rough table, and a cracker box for a stool, constitute my dining room and kitchen furniture. Vegetables are very scarce here, and we have but little to eat, except pork, beef and hard tack. We have much sickness among our troops, which I think is owing to the want of proper food and good water.

Yorktown seems to me to be a very unhealthy place, although it is situated high above the river, and has many ravines for drainage. The oldest inhabitants here seem to be subject to fever at certain seasons of the year

I am quite well, hoping to continue so, but I fear the accommodations of the camp will not agree with me. Write me soon, without fail, and believe me,

Yours truly, B. S. D. F.

To J. S. R., Albany, N. Y.

CAMP EIGHTY-FIRST REGIMENT, N. Y. VOLS.,
St. Helena Island, S. C., March 24, 1863

MY DEAR FRIEND—To-day is rainy, and everything is dull in camp, and it seems lonely and dreary, so I thought I would devote a few moments to you, informing you how things are down here in Dixie. Here I sit in my canvas house, all alone, with my great coat on, and feeling as cold as though it were a December day; still we have had weather here lately when the thermometer would mark ninety-eight in the shade, so great is the change.

While I am writing, the rain is pouring down in torrents, showing no mercy to the poor sentinel without, as he treads up and down his lonely beat. Very lucky for me that I have a good tent, with a fly over it, or I should get soaked through to the skin. Such days as these make me feel lonesome; but when the sunshine comes again I shall be happy, that is, as happy as we can be in the camp with army rations.

In these dreary hours the heart often flies back to its home, and the loved ones there. And how little those at home know the mysterious feelings that pass like a cloud over us; yet, in the silent hours of the night they come, and in the busy bustle of camp life, or in the silent retreats of solitude, overshadowing all the bright hopes and sunny feelings of the heart.

Who can describe, and who has not felt the bewildering influence of the heart; and still it is a delicious sorrow, and is like a cloud dimming the sunshine of the river, and causing a momentary shade of gloom to enhance the beauty of returning brightness, and fit us once more for the battle of life.

War is a terrible thing, and a civil war more than any other. How many hearts have been draped in mourning; and how many widowed tears have fallen for the loved ones slain? It really makes me feel sad when I think of it; and still it may all end for good.

I sincerely believe our cause is just and right, and he that is armed in a righteous cause is doubly armed. Although we endure hardships and privations, I still feel that the sacrifice is but small when compared with the blessings we shall achieve, for ourselves and our children, in maintaining and upholding the Union and the Constitution made by our fathers. God grant that we may never see them destroyed. Croakers at home may cry for peace, and discourage the weak; but I tell you that there can be no peace as long as there is a traitor in arms; and the Union army to-day fear the traitors and Copperheads at home more than Jeff Davis and his legions here. Only let there be a healthy sentiment at home, for a vigorous prosecution of the war, and I will guarantee that ninety days will finish up the rebellion. You may think I am sanguine on this subject, but I speak from what I have seen and what I know. You know that the aid which the Northern dough-faces have given to the rebels is tremendous, and I assure you that if we are defeated in putting down

the rebellion, the curse is on them, and not the Union
army, for the rank and file of the Union army are
loyal.   There may be a few traitors among the leaders,
but they are pretty well sifted, and the army to-day are
more united, and in better spirits, than they were a
year ago.

We soon expect to make an attack on Charleston,
and feel sanguine of success.   A simultaneous attack
by the army and navy will, I think, make that stronghold of rebellion tremble.   We may be defeated at
first, but it must eventually fall.   Oh, what a glorious
day that will be!   To see the Stars and Stripes floating
over the ramparts of Fort Sumter.   Here and at Vicksburg will be the death struggle of the rebellion.   If we
are successful in the capture of those two strongholds,
Davis & Co. will soon pack up their traps and leave.

This evening I received a letter from California; it
was from my brother, who wrote me he had enlisted
in a battalion of cavalry, which is to be sent North,
and attached to the Second Massachusetts.   I have
not seen him in over nine years.   There are now five
brothers of us in the service, which makes a very good
representation for one family.   I think if we all come
out of this struggle alive, we will be fortunate; but
this is more than can be expected.

Our Colonel is in command of our brigade, Acting Brigadier General. The brigade is composed of the Eighty-First New York, Twenty-Third Massachusetts, Ninety-Eighth New York, and Ninth New Jersey, making a very fine brigade, and we expect to do something big in the next fight.

We are within fifteen miles of Savannah, and fifty of Charleston. We can hear the guns of Fort Pulaski, which is garrisoned by a New York regiment. I think of taking a .trip down there in a few days, to see the fort and its surroundings.

Our regiment was never in better health. Remember me to all my friends. Write me on the receipt of this and I will keep you posted hereafter.

Yours truly,   B. S. D. F.

To J. S. R., Albany, N. Y.

CAMP EIGHTY-FIRST REGIMENT, N. Y. VOLS.,
MOREHEAD CITY, N. C., June 21, 1863

MY DEAR FRIEND—I have .answered yours of April 27th and have received none in reply. To-day the Colonel handed me a letter he received from you, which was sent by our Chaplain, in which you state

I had not answered your last. I have received two letters from you, both of which I answered promptly; your last may not have reached me; therefore I will while away a few minutes informing you how things are progressing down in old North Carolina.

This is the very heart of Dixie, both as to negroes and poverty. This portion of the State can never be any more than it is, on account of the poorness of the soil and shallowness of its waters. For fifty miles back from the sea shore it is all white sand, washed up from the ocean, and after a time it has produced shrubs and yellow pine, and these pine trees have afforded a living for the inhabitants, for the past fifty years, in manufacturing tar and turpentine. The trees are dying off and when they are gone the soil will be of little value; therefore, this part of the country can never be much.

The interior of the State, no doubt, is the granary from which the people of this locality are fed, for the country around us here cannot produce enough to sustain life; it is not in the soil to do it. Meadows and pasturage, which is so common with us at home, are not known here.

We are busy fortifying ourselves at this place, to prevent rebel raids down here. We are building a fort, on which will be mounted six guns, and a chain of rifle pits on either side of the fort, running to Bogue Sound and Calico creek. Those earthworks are of large dimensions, and I think will be capable, with the Eighty-First behind them, of resisting an attack of vastly superior numbers. We are here alone to guard Fort Macon, Beaufort, and this place, and I understand we are to be left here. Garrison duty is rather monotonous, not quite so much excitement as to be on the march, chasing an enemy, but, nevertheless, I think we have traveled around enough, and we should be satisfied, especially where we have the cool, refreshing sea breeze from the ocean to cool our heated blood, caused by the Southern sun.

We are having an awful thunder storm this afternoon; the rain is pouring down in torrents, and the wind blowing a tremendous gale, with thunder and lightning. A few days since I received a severe shock in my right arm, which I felt for some hours afterward; this is rather close quarters.

You, no doubt, as a loyal citizen of this glorious Republic, would like to know what this Department is doing toward crushing the rebellion. Well, I would say, we are at present acting on the defensive, trying to hold what we have got.

Many of the troops in this Department are nine months men, from Massachusetts, whose term of service is about to expire; therefore, we cannot advance much at present. But we are enrolling every white male citizen within our lines, and all negroes that come in, or are already in; they will form quite an army.

I cannot agree with some of my friends on this negro question. I do not believe that the negro is any better to face the enemy's bullet than a white man, nor do I fear they will be treated any worse than a white soldier, if the Government does its duty, which it must, at any sacrifice of rebel life. The negroes are willing to take up arms and fight under the old Stars and Stripes, with the prospect of their freedom, if we will protect them as soldiers; and if we use them as soldiers we must protect them as such, and if any of them are captured and hung by these slave traders, I say, take the same number, of equal rank, and hang them as you would a murderer. Let this once be understood, and we can enlist one hundred thousand negroes in the service of the United States. They will make good soldiers; I have seen many of them, and they compare well with the whites, as to drill and soldierly appearance, and they have the love of liberty planted as deep in their bosoms as most white men, and more than the white men of the South. And more than this, he should be recognized as equal with the white soldier, when they are engaged in one common cause. But when he lays off the blue jacket, he is a negro still, and should be treated as God designed he should be, as an inferior, with kindness and sympathy, but not as an equal, in a social point of view. These are my sentiments.

We have received papers of the 18th, by which I learn that the Rebs are in Pennsylvania. I hope they will reach some of the Copperheads, and make them feel the sore effects of invasion, and bring them to a sense of their duty. These vagabonds have prolonged this war by their peace doctrine; and now the rebels are invading Northern soil. This is the result of their infamous scheme for a dishonorable peace. I wish we could have every mother's son down here. I think we could take the peace out of them in three months, by making them do picket duty in the rivers and swamps of North Carolina, among the fleas and mosquitoes, under a burning sun.

Such men will be eternally cursed, for all time, by the soldiers of the Union army. I think if Vallandigham had been turned over to the soldiers, for punishment, he would have received his just deserts. He

18

would have been on his way to glory by this time. God is just, and will take him in his own good time. Be patient and firm.

Yours truly,   B. S. D. F.

To J, S. R. Albany, N. Y

EIGHTY-FIRST REGIMENT, N. Y. VOLS., }
FORT MACON, N. C., August 14, 1863. }

MY DEAR FRIEND—Your kind letter was received in due time, but I have not been able to answer it until now, owing to the multiplicity of business—going on raids and making out monthly returns, &c.

The Colonel received your letter last night, and in it you speak of my owing you a letter, which prompted me to a little extra exertion, and as I have just put my wife on board the steamer Guide, bound for home, I shall be more prompt to answer my friends, who think well enough to write to me.

Our last raid was on the Chowan river. We left our camp at night, and took the cars for Newbern; there we got on board steamers, went down the Neuse river, through Pamlico Sound, into Albemarle Sound, and thence up the Chowan river about sixty miles, to a place called Winton. We landed so quietly that the inhabitants were taken by surprise. The infantry, who numbered about two thousand, disembarked first. We then drew the artillery up by hand, not having any horses for them. The next move was to capture some horses, which was soon done, and on we went some five miles back in the country, the inhabitants fleeing to the woods. We had a few negro soldiers with us, who went out in advance, yelling like so many Indians, and firing in the air, which made the inhabitants believe it was a negro insurrection, which they dread more than anything else.

The houses that were found vacant had to suffer, as they were supposed to be owned by rebels. I captured a sabre and belt, the owner of which had just time to leave before we arrived. At another place we found an immense quantity of corn stored, which was designed for the Confederate service. We also found a large quantity of cotton and fodder, horses, negroes, &c., which were all taken. I found a fine young horse, whose master had abandoned him in his flight.

About three miles out we found a rebel camp, surrounded with rifle pits. They fired two volleys on our men, who made a charge and drove them out, and took possession of the camp and equipments; they left everything, even their guns. The same night we passed over the river about two thousand cavalry, who came from Suffolk to meet us. The next day they went within ten miles of Weldon, scouring the country, and had a little fight at Jackson, after which they returned with some two hundred horses and seventy prisoners. The cavalry again crossed the river and returned to Suffolk, and we returned to Newbern, with a load of cotton, two loads of negroes, and about three hundred horses. We were gone eight days, and came very near starving, as there was not much to eat in that vicinity. We lived most of the time on raw pork and hard tack. This was one of the tightest times we have seen in the service. The raids sharpen the appetite and make one tired, especially in hot weather.

I tell you in all truth, the rebels are hard up. We found them with but very little to eat, and such things as are common to us are almost impossible for them to get; for instance, coffee is $4 ⅌ ℔., flour $50 ⅌ barrel, common army shoes $25 ⅌ pair, a common straw hat $5, sugar $2 ⅌ ℔. This is so, for I have it from their own lips, and they all admit that the Confederacy has gone in. You can tell that by the cries of Jeff Davis in his last appeal to the Southern people.

Now for Charleston. Let the Government reinforce General Gilmore with white and black soldiers. Those

who know what they are fighting for, those who have
been on many a hard fought battle field, and those who
have felt the master's lash, are the ones to level that
stronghold; men who prize liberty and freedom above
their lives, not conscripts, that are bought up in the
market like so many sheep, and sent to be the com-
panions of brave men, who have endured the heat and
burden of the struggle.

To take Charleston requires steady and undaunted
courage, and before it is done our soldiers must wade
through rivers of blood. This is no small undertaking,
it will be a second Vicksburg, and, as I wrote you last
spring, the taking of these two places will bring on the
final death struggle of the rebellion. The taking of
Charleston will give us Savannah and Wilmington,
then what will Richmond be worth?

Our recent victories have darkened the hopes of the
Confederacy. The sky is dark for them, with hardly
one cloud that shows a silver lining; but with us is only
seen a speck here and there on the horizon. God grant
it may all soon be clear, and that every soldier in the
army may return to his home and family, is my earnest
and sincere desire. I hope a kind Providence will
guide the destinies of our armies in the field so that
every encounter may be a success to the Union cause,

until not a ray of hope is left to inspire the rebels in their wicked course. My prayer would be this even for the sake of humanity, if nothing else.

This war is a terrible thing; no man knows so well as he who participates in it. Think of the battle field• and hospital where thousands lie buried and wounded, then go back to the homes of these soldiers and see the misery there; the widowed wife and orphan children. I tell you it will not do to reflect upon. If I should allow my mind and sympathies to dwell on such things I should go mad, and every bugle note to war sounded would weaken my courage and unfit me for the sacrifice. This is no imagination, but a reality, and such feelings as these I find with our bravest soldiers, the most daring are also the most tender hearted.

What will become of our weak-kneed friends, the Copperheads, who will neither go themselves nor let others go? their destiny is written as visibly to my mind as the handwriting on the wall was to the old King at his feast.

Yours truly,   B. S. D. F.

To J. S. R. Albany, N. Y.

CAMP EIGHTY-FIRST REGIMENT, N. Y. VOLS., }
NEWPORT NEWS, VA., November 17, 1863 }

MY DEAR FRIEND—Your letter of the 9th came in due time, and as I am disappointed this morning in taking a ride to Warwick, on account of the blustering wind, so I will devote a short time in writing to you. Yesterday we had a review of our Brigade, which is composed of the Eighty-First New York Volunteer Infantry, Ninety-Eighth New York, Twenty-Seventh Massachusetts, Twenty-Fifth Massachusetts, Ninth New Jersey, Twenty-Third Massachusetts, with the Third New York Cavalry, one battery of Third Rhode Island Artillery, and a battery of the Third New York Artillery, making one of the finest brigades in the service. We are expecting to be ordered to the Potomac or Tennessee; however, this is mere surmise. In war time, you know, things are very uncertain, and the soldier has no choice as to where he is sent.

My own greatest desire is to have this rebellion put down, and return to old Albany, to enjoy once more the comforts of home life, for it is a great privation to be separated from society and the family. I often think of those pleasures and comforts which you are enjoying, while we poor fellows are trying to keep warm by a little fire in a canvas house, which is nothing more than a windbreak against the storm without. I think I shall never become accustomed to field life, and still I can stand it quite as well as the best of them. I see plainly that it tells on my constitution; the gray hairs begin to come.

Last Saturday I went over to Norfolk to spend the night. It was the first time in nine months that I had slept in a house. I had a good room and bed, but I caught cold in sleeping in such apartments. I could have taken a blanket and laid out all night, and felt better in the morning; this is the case with most of the soldiers; when they once become accustomed to living in tents, house accommodation unfits them for service.

It was really laughable to see the seedy gentlemen around the bar room; the so termed F. F. V's. Their coats were threadbare, and their hats were of a style worn at least ten years ago. Many of them wear the large, old fashioned collars, and swallow tailed coats. The hat, coat and collar made them look like "Dandy Jim from Caroline." No doubt they are the old clothes they cast off, when negroes sold more freely than at present, in the South. This place was once a great negro market. Poor old Virginia! how she has fallen from her high estate; her villages burned, her fields laid waste, and the blood of martyred brothers crying unto her from the ground. The day of retribution is at hand when her traitor sons will have to repent in sackcloth and ashes, or flee to the mountains for refuge, and call upon the rocks to hide them.

The news which reached us after election was glorious, and cheered every soldier's heart. We feel that our friends at home prize the sacrifice we are making. It gives us new life and faith that the North is loyal, and will stand by us through this conflict. You say the Union ticket is elected by 30,000 majority. That is glorious, but if the soldiers could have voted you would have seen 100,000 majority. Copperheadism is dead, and I hope it will be buried so deep that it will never know a resurrection.

We must stand by our country and sustain our Government. Do not let us falter or step back. Our radiant flag must be kept untorn, and floating to the breeze. Let not one star be stricken from its azure field, nor one memory lost of its glorious history. The cause of humanity and the hopes of freedom throughout the world are involved in this deathlike struggle for our nation's life. Let not our hearts grow cold or sympathies die out, for there is much earnest work to do. Let not patriotism be exchanged for gold or bartered for an inglorious peace, which mealy mouthed traitors are now trying to do. I hope the heads of Government will stand firm, and not be seduced by their wiles.

I am glad to hear that your business is good, and that old Albany is going along in the way of improvement. It is doing finely in the way of horse railroads; keep her going.

I wish you would visit us. I think it would pay you to come to Old Point Comfort. If you can I will furnish you with a blanket and a soft board to lay on. Your bones may feel sore for the first few days, but you will soon get used to it. We will give you hard tack and raw pork for a hasty dinner, and coffee without milk. You must not be negligent in writing; you see I am prompt.

Yours truly,   B. S. D. F.

To J. S. R. Albany, N. Y.

CAMP EIGHTY-FIRST REGIMENT, N. Y. VOLS., }
IN THE FIELD NEAR PETERSBURG, May 8, 1864. }

MY DEAR FRIEND—You will see by this that pen and ink is "played out," and Fourth of July soldiering is at an end for this campaign.

We left Yorktown on the 4th of May, with about thirty-five thousand troops, mostly veterans, on board of transports bound for some unknown point. We sailed down to Hampton Roads and anchored for the night. The next morning we put up the James river and landed at Bermuda Hundred, which is just above City Point, at the mouth of the Appomattox river, on which Petersburg is situated. The 18th Army Corps landed at this place, while the 10th Army Corps landed at City Point.

Our regiment has the extreme right of the 18th Corps, being the First Brigade of the First Division. We disembarked at dusk, moved out about a mile, and bivouaced in a wheat field. I rolled myself up in my blanket, in company with the rest of the field and staff officers, our horses lying by our side, ready for a march at a moment's notice. The night passed amid bustle and confusion, caused by the continual arrival of troops. At daylight we were ordered off toward Petersburg. Our regiment led the advance, and took a position about six miles out, where the bend of the James river makes the distance from the Appomattox only three miles. Across this point intrenchments are being made. We shall no doubt hold this place, as a base of operations, having gunboats in both rivers, which I believe will render our position secure, in case of a heavy force being thrown upon us.

I joined our regiment the following day, having been left to bring up our baggage, which consisted of a small valise for each officer. I took the advance of our wagon train, after having loaded my horse with nearly an hundred pounds of baggage, and started ahead. When about three miles out I was fired upon by a bushwhacker, who appeared to be concealed in the woods; the ball passed me and lodged in a tree; it made the limbs rattle. I however proceeded on my journey at a slow pace, and reached our regiment in safety. I have always felt more danger in following up the regiment in this way, than when directly with it, as the rebels are much given to lying in ambush for Quartermasters and their supplies.

This afternoon, which is Saturday, fighting commenced on our left. Three of our brigades were engaged, and took a high bluff, which commands the railroad to Richmond. Our boys made a charge on the rebels, and at first were repulsed; they rallied and drove the rebels, and now hold the road, and have torn up about four miles of it. Beauregard has arrived at Petersburg, with about twenty thousand men, from the South, who intend to obstruct our further advance.

I took my horse and rode out to the front, in company with the Colonel and Adjutant, and saw the smoke ascending, and heard the heavy booming of cannon and the rattle of musketry, which was within half a mile of us. General Butler and his staff were returning from the fight, and informed us that all was right, and said we had gained an important position.

Last night quiet reigned supreme. Nothing was heard save the measured tread of the sentinel, while here and there might be seen a single soldier seated by the expiring embers of a camp fire, thinking, perhaps, of the fondly remembered pleasures of home, from which he had torn himself to save his country from impending dissolution. How little do those at home know the soldier's feelings in the dreary hours of night. These are the hours for reflection.

The calm and quiet of last night is but a forerunner of a storm which is impending. No doubt a battle will be fought to-day; both armies are making vigorous preparations. The road is filled with ambulances going to the front, which is an indication of warm work ahead. God grant we may be victorious, and before the commemoration of o   National Anniversary I trust we will have the pleasu   to know that the rebel Capital has fallen, and that the glorious armies of the Union

19

have captured the rebel host, including Jeff Davis. This, so far, has been a successful expedition. Not less than seventy-five transports brought the troops up here, without a single accident occuring. We came very unexpectedly on Johnny Reb.; he seemed totally unprepared to receive us, giving us a fine opportunity to land all our troops.

I am writing this on a cracker box, under a burning sun, and the roar of artillery is heard in the distance. This being my third letter to-day, I begin to feel somewhat tired. You will excuse this hasty and imperfect sketch, but if you will answer more promptly I will hereafter give you a more vivid picture of the soldier's life in the field.

                    Yours truly,   B. S. D. F.

To J. S. R. Albany, N. Y.